Aval

Avalon Nights

SOPHIE DANSON

BLACK
lace

This edition first published in 1994 by
Black Lace
332 Ladbroke Grove
London W10 5AH

Reprinted 1995

First published as *Knights of Pleasure* in 1992
Copyright © Sophie Danson 1992

Typeset by TW Typesetting, Plymouth, Devon
Printed and bound in Great Britain by
Cox & Wyman Ltd, Reading, Berkshire

ISBN 0 352 32910 6

Prologue

*I*t was a stormy night. Heavy, snow-bearing clouds gathered on the horizon, presaging blizzards before dawn. Occasional flashes of lightning lit up the murky skies and revealed the castle keep, a mighty stone tower surrounded by a thick curtain wall. Impregnable to all enemies, all hostile forces; or so it seemed.

For this was the fortress of Camelot.

The night winds raged outside the Great Hall, tearing at the stone walls and howling at the windows as the first snowflakes began to swirl like murderous dancers on the frozen air. Inside, gathered around the Round Table, sat Arthur and eight of his most favoured knights.

They were troubled. For the wizard Merlin, Arthur's guardian since childhood and magical defender of the realm, had disappeared. Long weeks since, he had left Camelot; and none knew where he had gone. Only the waning power of his spells served as a warning that he was in danger: the magicai shield which he had cast up around the castle was growing weaker by the day. Soon Camelot would have no protection at all against the sorcery of its enemies and their evil magicians.

Somewhere, wherever he was, Merlin was in peril. And something must be done to save him.

'Pure Knights of the Round Table: I charge you watch and listen and mark me well. For tonight you shall learn truths that will terrify you: truths of the corruption that lurks deep within your souls.'

The voice cut through the smoky air like cold fire – searingly bright, and yet icy cold with an ageless, seductive evil.

The knights looked around them but at first saw nothing – only the dancing shadows on the cold stone walls, the prancing horses on the woven tapestries behind the dais that held Arthur's throne.

And then they saw it. A shape darker than the rest, at first formless, but which, as they watched, began to resolve itself into the figure of a tall woman, heavily veiled but naked save for a black velvet cloak spangled with silver and gold stars.

'Hold hard!' cried King Arthur, leaping to his feet and reaching for his trusty blade Excalibur. 'Who goes there, and what evil do you bring with you?'

The woman turned her head to face Arthur and, raising her arm, spoke again in the same chilling seductive voice: 'Be seated. You can do me no ill.'

At once, Arthur felt an immense force take hold of his shoulders and force him back into his seat. His knights, too, found themselves helpless to defend themselves, though they twisted and turned in their seats and tried to stand and reach for their swords. All they could do was gaze helplessly at the glorious nakedness before them, and lust after a touch, one more glimpse of those generous breasts, those hard brown nipples, those smooth, powerful thighs which could surely take any man within their compass and crush the life from his powerless body. Even a pure Knight of the Round Table.

'It is useless to struggle. You are in my power now. Your wizard Merlin cannot protect you.'

'What do you mean? Know you where Merlin is gone? Have you wrought your evil upon him?' cried Arthur.

'Look into the crystal, and you shall see.'

And the veiled woman placed in the centre of the table a large crystal globe. She passed her ringed hands over it several times, muttering words of power, and it seemed to the King and his knights that a cloud of mist was swirling in the depths of the crystal – a cloud which parted to reveal the images of two naked figures, disporting themselves on a pile of wolf pelts.

The female figure was naked save for her veil, and was sitting astride the naked male figure, whose vigorous penis was disappearing into her. She was riding him gleefully, and he was crying out with pleasure. As they watched, the knights saw his face become clearer and realised that they were looking at the face of a man in his middle years, powerful and lusty: the face of Merlin as they had last seen him.

As they watched, they saw the scene change. Now the male was on top of the female, lapping at her and thrusting two fingers into her womanhood. His face seemed to have aged, and there was grey in his hair.

Another scene, and another. And in each, Merlin seemed older, and less vital, until in the last he seemed transformed into a hideous old man, incapable of doing anything save lie beneath his lover and let her suck him to orgasm.

'What have you done, foul sorceress?' cried Galahad. 'What have you done to Merlin?'

'It is a trick,' cautioned the King. 'She shows us these images to trouble us, no more than that. Beware the wiles of women.'

'It is no trick,' replied the veiled woman. 'And if you will not believe these images, then you must believe the truth when it is brought before your eyes.'

She turned to face the door of the Great Hall and raised her arms. Forked lightning flashed from her fingertips and the door flew open. Wind and eddies of snow gusted through the hall. And in the midst of it all, standing in the doorway, was a small, hunched figure – little more than a wizened bundle clad in rags – leaning heavily on a stick.

'Merlin!' gasped the King, barely recognising his old mentor.

The wizened old man shuffled into the hall and raised his rheumy eyes to the veiled sorceress. When he spoke, it was in a cracked, worn-out voice: 'What is it that you would have me do, my Queen?'

'Stand before the King.'

The old man shuffled over to where the King was sitting.

'Merlin?'

'Touch him,' urged the sorceress, 'and you shall see that it is indeed he.'

And the King did so, and saw that this was indeed the magician Merlin, though scarcely recognisable; he had aged so terribly. His breath came in hoarse gasps and he could barely stand. The sorceress bade him sit, and he sank gratefully on to the steps of Arthur's throne, hands palsied and shaking.

4

'I have done what you asked, my beloved,' he gasped. 'Will you now suck my prick? It aches so for you.'

'Later. Tell the King how you came to be like this.'

'This mighty sorceress has enslaved me. She seduced me and became my mistress, and now she has enslaved my appetites and I am lost forever. Every time she slakes her lust upon my body I become a little weaker. My occult powers are almost all drained away now. And yet I cannot resist the exquisite bliss of feeling her kissing my manhood, sucking me dry, taking me into her hot, wet garden of delight.'

The King was appalled. 'And is there no way to save you? Is there no way to bring you back to me and restore your powers?'

'There is only one way,' replied the sorceress. 'I tire of my plaything, for he is almost spent now, and amuses me little. I am willing to accept the gift of another in his place. One of your knights may offer himself to be my lover. But mark me well: he must not offer himself lightly, for you have seen the consequences of my hunger for love. Whomsoever I take unto my bed will nevermore be seen again within these courts. And I shall drain the youth from his face, the sap from his loins.'

'I shall offer myself!' cried Sir Kay.

'And I!' The cries of self-sacrifice echoed through the Great Hall.

'Patience,' cooed the sorceress. 'Why, such an earnest desire to *die* in my arms! But there is another condition. *I* alone shall be the one who chooses my consort. And I shall select him in a particular way. This is what I command you to do. Each of you must tell the tale of your greatest sexual exploit. And that is the way in which I shall know which of you shall be my lover. Your poor magician will then be returned to you. But swiftly now! For time is short. See how he droops and withers before your eyes.'

'Let me begin!' cried Lancelot. 'For I would gladly sacrifice myself for my King and for Camelot. Let me tell the tale of my conquest of the beautiful Elaine, of how I saved her from a ferocious dragon and how in humble gratitude she begged me to take her body as a parting gift.' And he thought to himself: All shall be well, for I alone know the truth of the tale. Little white lies will turn the tale of my seduction into an unashamed celebration of my glory, and who but I shall ever know?

Little did he know what would befall him as he opened his mouth to speak the lie.

'Very well, Sir Lancelot. You may begin the tale. But before you begin, let me lay my hand upon your shoulder. I think you will find my touch lends you inspiration.'

And as the sorceress placed her hand softly upon Sir Lancelot's shoulder, he felt a tremendous surge of power pass through his body, as though lightning were seeking its way to earth through his flesh. He felt the sorceress's soft and sensual body pressing up against his back, and his penis rose to ramrod-stiff attention. But as he began to speak, he realised the terrible significance of the hand upon his shoulder, the power surging through his body.

He was unable to lie. It was impossible for him to tell anything but the unembellished truth.

The Story of Sir Lancelot and the Lady Elaine

When I was born, my arrival caused great consternation among the ladies of my mother's household. For, even at birth, my manhood was of extraordinary proportions. My poor mother, on seeing it, fell to weeping and swore that I should never be able to find myself a high-born wife willing to sacrifice her maidenhood upon my monstrous carnal lance. But my father and his men-at-arms laughed at such foolish fears, and swore I should conquer every woman – be she slut or noblewoman – that ever I desired.

Alas, as I grew older I began to realise that it was my mother's fears which held the greater part of truth. I was brought up with two female cousins who had been orphaned and had become my father's wards; and as I grew, I became more and more intimate with them, until at last, one day in my sixteenth summer, we fell to playing more dangerous games in my father's cherry orchard.

Aelgwyth was seventeen, and her sister Olave

sixteen; and although high born, they had received a broad-minded education from my father. He knew that, without dowries, they would be difficult to find good marriages for, and so – rather than foot the bill himself – he secretly hoped that one or other of them would get herself with child by some honest yeoman, and so become a farmer's wife, at no cost to himself. I knew that the girls were not virgins, for they often boasted to me of their exploits; and I could not help wondering what it would be like to couple with them – for I was already weary of my own virginity.

That hot, summer afternoon, we had been picking cherries in the orchard and were resting under one of the trees, our hands and mouths stained with the sweet juice of the ripe berries we had greedily sampled as we laboured. The villeins had gone to take their bread and cheese and ale, leaving us dozing – or so they supposed – in the orchard, alone and unsupervised.

As soon as we knew we were alone, our eyes sprang open and we fell to laughing and innocent horseplay. But as we frolicked, we grew bolder; and our sport became less innocent and more lewd.

'See!' cried Aelgwyth, bending her sister forward and pulling up her skirt. 'Two juicy peaches that we have forgotten to pick!' And she nibbled playfully at her sister's bare arse-cheeks – the sight of which filled me with the most tormenting lusts. I could feel the colour rising to my cheeks as my lusty young member reared its head within my leggings and begged leave to manifest its enthusiastic approval.

At length, Olave pulled away, near-helpless with laughter, and her hair tumbling over her white shoulders in blonde disarray.

'But what of these two fine pears?' she demanded, unlacing the front of Aelgwyth's bodice and pulling out two creamy bubbies, which, despite her tender years, were already full and appetising as two ripe fruits. 'Will no one taste these delicious fruits? Why then, I shall taste them myself!'

And Olave fell to sucking at her sister's ample breast, her fingers toying with the left nipple whilst her greedy mouth busied itself with the right. I noticed Aelgwyth's breath was quickening, and her feet were sliding very gradually further apart, as though she wished to make way for something.

As for me, my poor deprived manhood was striving to burst its way out of my hose, and only the unusual length of my doublet was protecting me from the sisters' prying eyes.

But alas, nothing could save me from discovery.

'Say, young Lancelot, have you no sweet delights with which to enthral and amaze us?' demanded the shameless Aelgwyth, who had now sat down opposite me and flung her legs wide apart. Since her skirts were kilted up to the knee to enable her to climb for the fruit, I was treated to a very fine view of young Aelgwyth's own bounty – a regular cornucopia of good things, crowded into the moist dark triangle between her appetising thighs.

'What would you have me show you?' I retorted, dry-mouthed and fearful – for I had permitted no woman or girl to see my manhood since I was old enough to dress myself. 'I have no such juicy pears, and my peaches are by no means impressive!'

'Sirrah, we seek the sight of that long, sap-filled bough that springs from between your legs,' replied Olave. And before I knew what was happening to me, the girls were upon me, tearing off my woollen leggings and exposing my most intimate sight to the unforgiving noonday sun.

There was a terrible silence, and then both girls shrieked and began to weep quietly.

'What ails you?' I asked, though I knew instantly what had made them cry.

'Never . . . never have I seen a prick of such length, such thickness!' cried Aelgwyth. 'I swear I cannot take it inside me, for it would split my tender young maidenhood like a ripe fig, and of such a wound as that would I most certainly never recover.'

'My sister tells you true,' assented Olave. 'For I tell you, my dear Lancelot, no noblewoman would ever submit herself to trial by such an ordeal as you bear between your thighs. Our mother told us when we were but babes that noblewomen have small and delicate parts, and a cock such as yours, dear Lancelot, would surely martyr our tender flesh.'

In a rage of disappointment, I gazed down at my manhood, cursing it for its unnatural proportions. Why must I be cursed with such a monstrous deformity? Why, I might never ever find any woman who would take it into her. And I fell immediately into a terrible depression.

Fortunately, the sisters were resourceful and did not intend leaving me to suffer the agonies of my unsatisfied prick. No, they had other plans for me.

They laid me on my side, and Aelgwyth knelt facing my front, Olave my backside. Then they began to play with me most deliciously, bringing forth from me groans of instant pleasure.

Aelgwyth took me joyfully in hand, and pumped my shaft with such vigour that her naked bubbies bounced upon her chest in a most wonderful fashion. I toyed with them, rolling their nipples between my finger and thumb and sucking at them as though I were some tiny helpless babe. Meantime, Olave inserted a hand between my arse-cheeks and began the most lewd exploration imaginable of the forbidden territory between bollocks and arsehole. How I blushed and cried out and shivered with delight as I felt her sharp-nailed index finger suddenly jabbing its way through my forbidden gate.

With cries of joyful release I came, shooting my seed all over Aelgwyth's hands and bubbies. And we lay locked together, all three, for a long time, panting and giggling with the stolen pleasure of the moment – until at last the girls sprang to their feet and announced that they were to demonstrate to me exactly how a woman frigs herself.

And oh! how wonderful it was to see their legs spread wide apart, their fingers on their clitorises, burrowing into entrances front and rear, their hands tormenting already-stiffened nipples into ever-greater hardness.

But how I wished they would take me inside them; that my manhood was acceptable to them. For I so longed to lose my virginity inside a woman's well-lubricated hole.

A week later, a common wench who served my father at table stopped me as I passed the barn where she was busy gathering eggs for supper.

'Good morrow, young sir,' she smiled. And I could not help thinking what pretty lips she had, what pretty titties and hips and thighs.

'Good morrow, Freya,' I replied, embarrassed to find my cock already crowing at such a fair sight. 'What are you doing?'

'Why, I'm collecting eggs, sir,' she replied. 'But it is such a dismal business, you know, sir; and I can't

11

help thinking as how I'd prefer a nice tumble in the straw with you.'

I was flabbergasted by her forwardness, but not a jot daunted. If anything, my prick swelled even more to hear her talk such filth. But a twinge of sadness clutched at my soaring heart. Surely, the minute she saw the size of my weapon, she would decline to join the fray.

Nevertheless, I dismounted from my pony, tethered it by the barn, and followed Freya inside into the cool darkness where the only sounds were of chickens scurrying about on the straw. The place was filthy and smelt of chicken dung; but what did I care? Perhaps in this semidarkness she would not notice my oversized cock until it was too late.

As soon as we were inside the barn, Freya turned her back to me and bade me release her from her clothes. I fumbled tremblingly with the fastenings of her coarse woollen gown, and at last succeeded in unlacing her. Impatiently, she shook my untutored hands from her and pulled the gown, and her linen shift, down over her hips, stepping out of them where they lay upon the barn floor.

She turned to me and smiled at me as only country girls can – an open, honest smile that is no more than it seems: the expression of a straightforward offer. And, as Freya's offer matched my need, I hastened to cast off my own clothes before her. Yet at the back of my mind was that same fear which had haunted me since childhood and which had so recently been reinforced by my experiences with Aelgwyth and her sister Olave.

I struggled out of my tabard, shirt and riding boots, leaving only my hose. And already, I was anticipating the young woman's dismay, her excuse, her refusal . . . her flight. But I sensed that I could not stop now; for my prick was throbbing like the heart of some mighty beast, and I knew that I must have the girl. I knew, too, that it was not dark enough to conceal my nature and purpose from Freya's keen young eye. She would see my prick in all its glory – and I must simply take my chance with her reaction.

To my immense delight, as my mighty weapon sprang into view, Freya gave a great cry of delight:

'Oh my lord, what a beautiful instrument you have, to be sure!' she cried, falling upon her knees and covering it with the most devoted kisses. 'Is it not a mighty weapon? The mightiest I have ever seen. Why, a dainty lady might fear to be split in two with such a lance!'

'But . . . you?' I stammered. 'You are not afraid to lie with me? Are you not afeared lest I should also split you in two?'

Freya laughed prettily, and shook her head:

'A low-born lass, be she dairymaid or whore, is well practised in the arts of the long grass and the hayrick, schooled to the sport since first she could suck a prick. But 'tis my belief that your high-born noble lady has such a terrible fear of the prick that she will take only the little ones, as will fit into her without effort. Poor, deluded ladies: they know not the pleasure of being filled to the brim and amply greased with pleasure-juices. They fear that a big fat cock such as yours, my lord, would hurt them: and to be sure, I fear they may tell true. For they are built so delicate and so fragile, I feel sure their lower lips must be as tight-sewn as their little rosebud mouths.'

And she pulled my mouth down to hers and kissed me; and I felt the great soft mass of her generous

13

mouth, and prayed that the lass would be as amply endowed in her nether parts. At last! At last I had found a woman who would take me inside her belly with joy, and not with fear.

Freya fell backwards, laughing, on to the straw, and pulled me down on top of her. Joyfully, I let myself overbalance and – without further ado, for I was very young and my cock had a hasty will – I buried myself to the hilt in her delicious moist warmth.

Despite Freya's cheerful assurances, my cock only just fitted into her hole, and the deliciously tight fit set my head spinning with pleasure. I thrust into her, very hard, and felt her answering thrust. I was giving her pleasure! I, who had thought never to know that joy!

And I rode her greedily to orgasm, knowing such pleasure that, being but a youth, I was within moments ready to ram into her once again – and this time, with one hand between her legs and the other squeezing her soft breasts, I brought Freya to a mighty crisis of passion, in which she dug her nails into the flesh of my back as my seed burst forth a second time from my youthful loins.

From that day, I vowed that never henceforth would I ever lie with any gentlewoman or high-born lady; for I knew I could not bear the humiliation of her rejection. I vowed that I would lie only with low-born women, those women who had ridden many cocks so that they would welcome the hot, hard thrust of my own massive weapon.

But little had I reckoned with the wiles of the Lady Elaine.

Ten years from the day on which Freya brought me to manhood, I had occasion to spend several nights at the manor of Adenthorpe, in the North

14

Lands where His Majesty the King had but lately brought his laws to bear upon the unruly populace.

Adenthorpe had been bestowed by the King as a gift upon Sir Bors, one of his most trusted knights, whose wife – the Lady Elaine – was renowned throughout the kingdom as a beauty. Not that my Lady Elaine's loveliness was of any great interest to me: for I had forsworn all high-born ladies.

On the first evening, my companions and I feasted richly on swan and wild boar at Sir Bors's table, whilst the Lady Elaine and her ladies-in-waiting ate in the solar, where it was thought more fitting for them to be, out of the sight of rude, men-at-arms. I could not suppress a pang of regret that I had glimpsed this beautiful lady only briefly, and that even then I had been able to see her only through the veil which she wore to protect her from covetous eyes, in deference to her jealous husband's wishes.

My days at Adenthorpe passed agreeably enough, except for one thing: Sir Bors was a man of excessive moral rectitude – a man who believed that fornication was the worst of all sins, and who would not hesitate to kill any man who so misbehaved within the precincts of his manor.

But I, as you know, am a man of hot desires and lusts which I needs must satisfy as often as I can. It was not that I meant to dishonour any gentlewoman or respectable lady, I simply craved to lie with one of the dairymaids, or the common slut who sweeps the kitchen floors – or even a passing whore, who wanders from village to village, offering her services in return for bread and shelter for the night. But the noble Sir Bors would have none such within the pale of his homestead; and I began to believe that I should burst for the lack of release, if I did not die of boredom first.

And then, on the third evening, I received the most curious little note. It read:

'Sir Lancelot: know you that I am not of one mind with my husband. I believe that knightly virtue should be celebrated and rewarded, not repressed. I know you to be the best knight in the whole kingdom of Camelot. If you will do me the honour of coming to my chamber at midnight, you shall know the warmth of my welcome.'

I realised the enormous dangers which the Lady Elaine must have placed herself in to send this note to me, and it was with genuine regret that I wrote this reply:

'My Lady Elaine: I receive your offer with the deepest warmth and gratitude. But, alas, I cannot accept. For, as you will discover if you make enquiries about me, I keep company only with low-born women and harlots. Never would I seek to dishonour a high-born lady as yourself. I am your most devoted servant, Lancelot.'

I sent the note to Elaine with the same lass who had brought it to me: a rather plain lass, but one with whom I would gladly have taken my comfort had she been willing to offer herself to me. Her haste to leave me made me realise how thoroughly the worthy Sir Bors had instructed all his female servants to shun the ways of the flesh. I began to regret keenly my decision to rebuff the Lady Elaine, though I knew that I must not break my vow, if only for the sake of my own sanity.

But all was not lost. That very evening another note arrived from the Lady Elaine. This time, it promised a much more acceptable solution to my difficulty.

'My dear Sir Lancelot: I have made enquiries about you, and I entirely understand your difficulties. I therefore take no offence at your rebuttal. But I should be honoured if the best knight in the land would allow me to show my admiration of him in another, more acceptable way.

'If you come tonight to my private chapel, you will discover awaiting you there four young wenches who will, I believe, meet your every requirement. Their only reservation is that they desire to be masked, so that their lord Sir Bors will never know what they have done in defiance of his wishes.

'Send your reply with the girl who brings this note. You can trust her absolutely.'

I thought for a moment about the implications of what I had just read. What if I was walking into a trap prepared for me by the jealous Sir Bors, to determine whether I really was the chaste knight I pretended to be? Was it not most audacious and foolish of the Lady Elaine to have written to me in this way? And yet, I knew that I would not be able to resist. So I scribbled my reply on the back of the note which she had sent to me: 'I shall be there.'

I made my apologies – claiming that I was fatigued – and went early to bed, but did not undress or sleep, afraid as I was that I would miss the appointed hour. Just before midnight, I arose from my bed and crept down the back stairs of the house to the Great Hall, where some of the servants lay sleeping on the rush-strewn floor. To my great relief none awoke; though one of the dogs raised its head and gave a little low growl as I passed.

Safely through the Great Hall, I slipped behind the curtain which shielded it from the solar, and through that deserted room to the passage which led to my Lady Elaine's private chapel.

Opening the great wooden door, very carefully so as not to make a sound, I peered into the chapel beyond. At first glance, it seemed deserted, save for the few candles left burning beside the altar, to the memory of knights killed in recent battles. But as my eyes grew accustomed to the gloom, I realised that some of the shadows were moving. And they were not shadows at all, but the shapes of naked women, moving out of the gloom and processing towards the chapel door to greet me.

Hurriedly, I slipped inside and closed the doors behind me. The women were before me now, and I saw that they were indeed masked. I counted five, not four, as the Lady Elaine had promised; and thanked my lucky stars for such a beneficent patron.

There were two blondes, a brunette, a redhead and a girl with waist-length hair pulled back in a jet-black, glossy plait. All were well formed and young, and I could feel the sap rising in my loins already.

'Greetings, Sir Lancelot,' breathed the brunette, a slender but shapely lass with a soft country burr which stirred my prick to feverish activity within my hose. 'We are summoned here by our mistress, the Lady Elaine, to do all your bidding.'

'What is your will, my lord?' demanded one of the blonde girls, unfastening her hair so that it fell in waves about her bare shoulders. Her voice was soft but commonplace: the voice of a practised doxy who is no longer cowed by the substance of her trade.

For a moment, I was lost for words. So many choices, so many glorious bodies offering themselves up for my pleasure – good, honest wenches who would not baulk at my manhood. And I felt an immense surge of gratitude towards my benefactress, the Lady Elaine, who had showered such bounty upon me without a thought of her own gain.

And that thought brought me to my senses, and reminded me that, since Elaine had shown such generosity towards me, I should reciprocate by making the most of that I had been given. I turned to the red-haired girl and stroked her chestnut ringlets gently.

'It is my will that you, girl, should undress me; and that, while you are undressing me, I should have the leisure to let my fingers and tongue wander wherever they will upon and within your body.'

'Your will is my desire,' replied the girl; and something in her voice told me that she was smiling. My cock grew impatient within my hose at the thought of such mutual pleasure-giving.

I sat down upon a carved oak chest, and the red-haired girl began to open my doublet, which fastened down the front by means of buttons carved from semi-precious stones: amber, jasper, jade, agate and amethyst. They gleamed seductively against the black velvet of my embroidered doublet. Slowly and carefully, the girl peeled back the two sides of the garment and I slipped my arms out of it.

Immediately, my fingers sought fitting recompense for such forward behaviour, seeking out intimate places to torment and titillate. The girl was bending forwards from the waist to fumble with the strings of my shirt, and my hands fell naturally to playing with her bubbies, which were small and firm, with little rosebud-pink tips which demanded to be tasted.

I weighed these twin delights in my hands, felt their firmness and was surprised at their weight. Then I pulled the girl further down towards me and took one of her nipples into my mouth, at first licking and sucking at it and then beginning to bite gently upon it. This first contact of my teeth upon her tender flesh caused the girl to squeal with surprise and pain; but after the initial shock had worn off, and the warmth began to spread through her body and awaken her loins, she fell to moaning quietly as she tugged ever more frantically at the stubborn strings of my shirt.

At last the strings yielded, and reluctantly I allowed her to draw away from my lips in order to pull the shirt off over my head. She immediately began to kiss my bare flesh and to admire my well-muscled arms and broad chest.

Whilst she was so busied, I took the opportunity to slide my hand between her thighs and then upwards, so that the edge of my hand slotted precisely into her intimate furrow. She was dripping with wetness. Truly she was that best of all harlots: the woman who excels at her work because it gives her such great pleasure.

As I rubbed my hand lewdly along her crack, the girl began to move her hands down from my chest to my waist, and so to the drawstring which held my black silken hose tight around me. I knew that, even in the gloom of the candlelit chapel, the girl must already have felt the huge outline of my swollen penis as it strove for release from its prison; and I was well satisfied to see that her realisation had in no wise diminished her eagerness to undress me.

As an incentive to make the girl hurry, I began to toy lewdly with her most intimate parts: forcing apart her thighs with my hands so that she stood before me with legs splayed and titties hanging down – a perfectly submissive, yet delightfully inventive wench.

Next, I set to exploring the moist delights which peopled her crack; and soon found my fingers straying to two holes: one very tight and quite dry, the other capable of infinite expansion and as wet as a mighty river. I felt the girl give a start of extreme pleasure as I burrowed my thumb into her lake, and my index finger into her dry well, so that I had her prisoner on a double lance.

With much delicious malice, I used the index finger of my right hand to explore the territory around the moister hole, giving a cry of triumph as I found what I was looking for – a fleshy mound, larger than most of those I had felt before, and throbbing for all it was worth with the pulse of this eager courtesan's desires.

Almost distracted by her lusts, the girl tore frenziedly at my hose, but I had determined that I would offer her no assistance – after all, my hands were already gainfully occupied elsewhere. I rubbed at the girl's clitoris, and jabbed my finger and thumb in and out of her, provoking her to the most entertaining divagations.

'Oh, oh, my liege, my lord!' she cried. 'I will do anything, anything! I will stick my tongue up your arse, or you shall take me howsoever you will, only make me come, make me come!'

At that moment, the girl at last succeeded in releasing my prick from its prison. She tore down my hose and my cock leapt forth in triumph, crowing its desire for all to see. Instead of the shrieks of terror to which I had grown accustomed, I heard only moans of feverish desire as the women clustered round in their eagerness to be first to sample my massively engorged manhood.

But I had unfinished business with the red-haired girl, who was crying out her desire loudly now, entranced by the sight of my mighty penis. Working my fingers ever-faster inside her, I applied just the right amount of pressure to her clitty and lo! I felt the waves of pleasure crashing through her.

I took away my hands, and the girl slumped to the ground, panting and almost fainting away. The fragrance of her orgasm was on my fingers, driving me almost crazy with desire for these masked women, who clustered about me in the gloom of the chapel like perverse nuns, maddened by an excess of religious zeal. Indeed, it did seem to me that their devotion to my prick was a form of idolatry; for they were now all upon their knees, vying to see who might shower it with the most tender kisses, the most exciting caresses.

'Fear not, ladies!' I cried. 'For my sexual powers are as great as is the size of my cock – there is seed aplenty to fill all your mouths and hidden grottoes; and whosoever tires of the sport before dawn, I wager it shall not be me!'

The women seemed much cheered at this news, which was quite true: for I have always had potency to match the great size of my organ and the generous stones which flank it. Oft have I worn out a half-dozen harlots before midnight, and still had to masturbate twice to rid myself of unclean thoughts before I could retire to my bed and drift off into a peaceful slumber.

As though to prove the truth of my boast, I immediately took hold of my cock and masturbated in front of the ladies – an operation which took but a few moments, since I had abstained too long from carnal gratification, and had in any case been provoked to the brink of orgasm by my dalliance with the red-haired whore. To make my joy complete, I knelt over the still-prone body of the red-haired girl as I rubbed my mighty cock, thrilling at the sight of sticky white semen sprinkling her face and breasts as I came, with a roar of pleasure, to orgasm.

Immediately my seed had spurted forth, I felt my cock grow even stronger and more eager than before – and I looked for a new partner to gratify me a second time. It came to me all of a sudden that it would be amusing and agreeable to see the lasses lap up my seed from their sister's body, so I commanded them:

'On your knees! I want to see you lick up all my semen. On your knees like bitches in heat!'

Willingly, the girls fell to their knees, and set to lapping up the copious quantities of my seed that had fallen upon the red-haired girl's naked body. Even though they were masked, I could tell from their hoarse, quickening breathing, that they found my command both agreeable and exciting.

I, for my part, took advantage of the girls' helplessness to explore their bodies a little more closely. My cock – which was once more nigh on a cubit's length and the thickness of a woman's wrist – was dancing about wildly, and begging for entrance into one of the gloriously juicy orifices which were offering themselves to me.

'Oh take me, take me!' cried the girls, thrusting out their backsides to me, the better to offer their sweetness up to me. Only the black-haired girl remained silent, as though she were afraid that if she spoke, her voice would betray her. But, maddened with desire as I was, I thought nothing of it. Indeed the silence and grace of the dark-haired harlot only served to render her even more desirable in my eyes; and I resolved that I would save her until the last, that she should receive my most abundant tributes.

The brunette was the next to take my fancy, and I determined that I would surprise her. Pulling apart her arse-cheeks, I placed the tip of my weapon not against the entrance to her sex, but against her puckered brown arsehole. Despite her squeals of fear, I anointed the target with a little of her own juice and rammed into her, with scarcely a thought for the discomfort which I must surely be causing her.

The poor girl's arse was stretched tight; but I succeeded in entering her, and the difficulty proved well worthwhile. The inside of the girl's arse felt like a tight velvet glove upon my hot and throbbing penis, and my own pleasure soon communicated itself to the girl, who began to gasp with desire and thrust herself back against me, as though hungry for me to run her through with yet more inches of my mighty lance.

I felt my crisis approaching, and finished her off with a few strokes of my fingers upon her clitty. We fell to the ground in a disordered heap, panting and heads spinning with the unbelievable pleasure of our shared experience. For the first time in my life, I was beginning to enjoy my oversized cock and the un-usual sexual stamina which accompanied it. I rolled over, on to my back, and waited for my cock to recover.

Whilst I was still lying there, my prick swelling back to its former magnificance, I felt a gentle touch upon my thighs: and opening my eyes, I saw that the two blonde girls were kneeling beside me, licking me with soft velvet tongues. I bade them continue and lay back to enjoy their ministrations. The girls soon provoked me to a frenzy of desire, for the touch of their tongues upon my stones was the most delightful sensation I had ever experienced.

Feeling that I could wait no longer, I commanded one of the girls to sit astride my belly, facing my feet, with my erect cock rubbing between her thighs but not buried inside her. I then commanded the other blonde girl to sit atop the first. In this way, my massive cock was able to stimulate both of them simultaneously, whilst also giving me the greatest pleasure – particularly as the second blonde girl was able to masturbate me with her hand.

Our ride was breathless and thrilling – a dizzying tumble into ecstasy as the girls reached their climax and I shot my semen all over their waiting bellies.

This left only one of the women who had not yet received the benefits of my undivided attention: the dark-haired girl who had bewitched me with her silence. I turned to her and bade her come to me, and she obeyed. Kissing her breasts, I noticed that her skin was whiter and softer than the other girls', and that her hands were not callused and worksore. Perhaps I should have been suspicious; but I merely assumed that this was some higher-class courtesan – perhaps even a girl that the saintly Sir Bors kept secretly for his own pleasures. In which case, I told myself, I would enjoy her all the more for knowing that I was stealing his treasures from him.

Before I had given much thought to what I would demand of the girl, she was on her knees between my thighs, sucking the tip of my prick with obvious relish. But I did not want to spend my seed thus: so, pushing her off a little roughly, I forced her to lie on her back on the ground, and – desperate with hunger for her – pressed the tip of my prick against the girl's sex.

To my surprise, the girl was tight – much tighter than any I had ever lain with in my life. And she gave a little moan of obvious pain as I began to press home my weapon. But she showed no signs of reluctance to take me into her, and if anything, this tightness served only to excite me. With a great thrust, I entered her, stretching her and causing her to cry out in discomfort.

And yet she was wetter also than any woman I had ever lain with, and clearly as hungry for me as I was for her. Within moments of entering her, the juices of her desire had soothed away her pain and were making my passage easy.

I rode her hard, as I would my warhorse; and she responded with eager thrusts of her hips, taking into her belly every inch of my manhood that it would hold. And when I came to my pleasure, she came with me, crying out with joy and clasping me to her, as though she were reluctant to let one precious drop of my seed escape from her gloriously tight passage.

I rode her many more times that night, and each time I begged her for her name; but she would not speak, and only shook her head, sadly or so it seemed to me.

At dawn, I parted company with the five girls who had so expertly pleasured me through the night; and, still masked they left me to make my own way back to my apartments.

I wanted to thank the Lady Elaine, but her ladies-in-waiting told me that she was indisposed, and could not see anyone. The following day, I was bidden to ride back to Camelot, there to give account of myself to the King. As I was riding out, a messenger hurried up to me and gave me a message, with strict instructions not to open it until I was at least a day's ride from Adenthorpe.

I obeyed his instructions, and thought no more of

the missive until I was back at Camelot, where I opened it and read the following:

'My dear Sir Lancelot: since you would not take me as a lady, you must needs take me as a whore. For a prophecy was made upon the day of my baptism; a prophecy which foretold that I must bear a son by the best knight in the land – for that son would grow to excel even his own father, and would one day become mightier than Arthur himself. This is why I tricked you into lying with me. And yet that is not the only reason: for I desired you above all men, and I have known supreme pleasure with you.

'Think not too ill of me, for you were the joy of my loins, and none shall ever equal the pleasure which you gave me, your dark-haired whore.'

At first I was angry, for I had been cruelly tricked – and I feared greatly the prophecy concerning the child. And yet, I had known great pleasure with the Lady Elaine. And that fact in itself was my consolation: for if one high-born lady had been willing to take my cock inside her, why not many others?

And that is when my thoughts first turned to the Lady Guinevere . . .

Sir Gawain

'*B*etter and yet better,' hissed the veiled woman, her fine features shadowy behind the black gauzy curtain. Her eyes, almost obscured by the dark veils, glittered with a faraway menace, a defiant glee. 'My dear Sir Lancelot, can it be that so noble a knight could be so easily tricked by a mere chit of a girl?'

Lancelot blushed crimson to the roots of his hair, his mind a maze of utter confusion. For he had meant to tell a very different tale: an untrue tale of dragons and maidenly gratitude, devised expressly to glorify his part in it; and yet, when he had opened his mouth to speak, a great compulsion had washed over him like spring tides, forcing him to confess the truth of his fears and failings before his mocking peers. He saw their pitying half-smiles, and wished the earth would swallow him up.

In a frenzy of rage, he leapt to his feet and reached for his sword. 'Reveal your face, evil witch!' he cried, his hand upon the sword-pommel. 'Or die!'

And he clutched at the sword and made as though

to swing it high up above his head, the better to bring its hungry blade slicing down upon his tormentor. But the harder he gripped the hilt, the less it would yield – it was stuck faster in its scabbard than Excalibur in its enchanted stone.

'Hold fast, Sir Lancelot!' laughed the veiled temptress, her mocking laughter shaking her full breasts invitingly, tormentingly as she stood before him and dared him to strike her down. 'What: can you not lift your sword, good Sir Knight? Art thou grown feeble as a lass, too feeble to resist the frail white flesh of a mere woman?'

And she began to caress his penis through his hose, tracing its massive outline with a pointed red talon as a ravening beast might toy with its prey in the moment before it pounced to bite, rend, tear, consume its sweet tender flesh. No matter how he tried to struggle away from her, Lancelot found his hands held fast: his right hand clenched unwillingly on his sword-pommel, and the left fixed in frustrated immobility to the wooden tabletop. His hands felt leaden-heavy and numb. He realised that he was completely helpless.

Lancelot was mortified to feel his huge manhood fluttering into life at her divinely evil touch. He looked down and saw it swelling, bulging the front of his hose, growing heavier and harder and more alive with every tormenting caress. The shame, the humiliation . . . And yet, the pleasure, the sublime pleasure of those delicate caresses. This strange, alien woman was playing upon him as a minstrel plays upon a lute – delicately, knowingly, with infinite power.

'No more!' he cried, but the words dried to dust in his throat, and only a hoarse croaking issued forth from his lips. And in truth he did not wish her to stop caressing him. He wished only for her to exploit his powerlessness, to go on using him as Elaine had used him, to go on giving him this same, exquisite pleasure for ever. At that moment, Lancelot wanted nothing in the whole universe beyond the exquisite touch of this veiled temptress's skilled fingers upon his swollen penis.

He did not even yearn for her to pull down his hose and lay her fingers upon the bare flesh of his shaft; for the very touch that she was bestowing upon him was Heaven itself – the sliding of the coarse woollen fabric across the bare tip of his erect prick made him shiver with the most acute pleasure, so refined that it was almost pain. He forgot completely that all eyes were upon him, that his reputation as an honourable knight was in tatters. He cared for none of it, not now. All he wanted was for this state of utter blessedness to go on for ever.

But it was not to last.

'Sit ye down, good Sir Lancelot!' urged the woman, her own voice heavy with honeyed malice. 'The night is yet young. The moon is newly risen and the revels are just begun. There are many other stories to tell, many other confessions to hear.'

And she raised her arm and pointed her ringed finger at Lancelot, who felt his limbs grow still heavier until at last he sank reluctantly into his chair, his penis still rebellious and achingly erect. But he knew that his tormentor would offer him no comfort.

The sorceress paced the cold stone floor, her generous stiff-nippled breasts thrusting forward and parting the starry fabric of her midnight-black cloak, flashes of her milky thighs disturbing the tranquillity of all who saw her. The knights waited, expectant and excited now, to see what would happen next.

Suddenly she stopped, and turned so that her back was to the knights.

'I call upon the knight who is known as Gawain,' she breathed. The words fell like rain that freezes even before it touches the earth.

Gawain felt his blood freeze. What horrible fate might lie in store for him? And yet, if she called upon him to tell some salacious tale, surely he could escape the ignominy simply by lying? He relaxed a little, and rose to his feet, addressing the sorceress in a clear and confident voice.

'What is it that you want of me, mysterious lady?'

There was heavy irony in the sorceress's voice. 'Sir Gawain, I think we are all weary of Sir Lancelot's tale of his frailty in the face of feminine wiles. I wish, therefore, that you should tell me some tale of strength. You are a powerful knight, well formed and pleasing to the eye. Have you, perhaps, some more diverting tale to tell? Some spicy tale of dishonour?'

'My lady, I am an honourable knight. Yes, I have tales to tell you of my prowess with the fair sex, but how could an honourable knight have tales to tell of dishonour? For you must know that no true-hearted knight of the Round Table would stoop so low as to do harm unto a lady's virtue.'

The sorceress was standing behind him now, her curiously cold breath chilling the hairs on the back of his neck. He felt oddly as though she were seeing directly into his mind: it was a caressing, a delving, a gentle tearing down of his every barrier. And he felt his prick twitching at the memory: the memory of a very beautiful, very pure ice maiden whom he had once taught to catch fire. Taught in his own special way . . .

The sorceress was so close now that he could feel

her naked flesh pressing against his back. Her hand was on his shoulder, and her lips were brushing his ear. She was talking to him, so quietly that only he could hear. A voice that echoed through his mind, and he realised with horror that she had the power to unmask him: that this night he must lay bare his soul before his comrades in arms.

'Speak, Sir Gawain,' breathed the voice in his ear. The candles seemed to flare brighter as the mingled terror and excitement took hold of him. 'I compel you to tell the tale of the Lady Oruale. And know this: that you must tell the truth, or perish.'

Gawain opened his mouth to speak, to say something – anything – that would chase away the story he so feared to tell; but as his lips formed the lie, it was as though the life's breath was strangled in his throat; as though cold hands were tightening about him, threatening to squeeze the life from him as easily as he might wring the neck of a wounded bird. As easily as his hands had wrung pleasure from the unwilling body of the Lady Oruale . . .

As soon as he began to speak the truth, the invisible hands began to relax; and, fearful of a renewed assault, Sir Gawain began to tell the tale of his shame.

THE TALE OF SIR GAWAIN
AND THE LADY ORUALE

The castle of Orud-Ddur lies on the borders of Wales, far distant from Camelot. It is a wild and fearsome land in which only a skilful warrior may survive. Masterless men roam the verges of these desolate marchlands, and there is no law save the law of the sword.

And into this hostile land was brought the Lady Oruale: a pale and perfect ice maiden from the North Lands, a Viking princess with golden hair and the purest, whitest skin – a prize for any princeling. She was bought to wife by Sir Bercilak, newly installed as overlord of Orud-Ddur, and as such the vassal of my lord the King.

But Oruale was no fragile flower. She was a breathtaking ice maiden with a heart of burning cold fire. She had been the daughter of a king, and to be married to a young knight with a poor domain in a wild and uncivilised country was, to her, the greatest dishonour. And so she closed her heart to him and made up her mind to deny him all save what she could not refuse to give.

And so it was that the Lady Oruale, married three months to her young and eager husband, was yet a virgin when I came upon her: a virgin with a cold heart and without carnal desires – or so it seemed at first sight.

My lord Arthur sent me to Orud-Ddur as his general, to inspect the lands and fortifications of his new vassal Sir Bercilak. I rode many days and nights until I reached his castle with my four men-at-arms. We had faced an ambush and several bloody skirmishes, and were tired and sore when we reached Orud-Ddur at dusk on the tenth day of our journey.

But I was at once revived when I set eyes upon the lovel Oruale. She was tall and slender, blue-eyed and with a great mane of smooth, flaxen hair gathered into a long plait which fell forwards across her shoulder and followed the enticing curve of her swelling bosom, close-confined in its tight bodice.

I at once desired the woman; but, mindful of my own and the woman's honour, I sought to put such

33

thoughts from my mind. And yet, I could not forget that look of icy indifference, which, paradoxically, inflamed my own desires all the more. The thought of putting fire into that filly's cold belly filled me with the most exquisite longings, which I feared I must never satisfy.

A good night's sleep restored me to health and strength, and I set about my lord's business. The first day was spent in a meticulous inspection of Sir Bercilak's lands and castle. I saw nothing of the Lady Oruale until the evening, when she appeared like some unearthly vision at the head of the dinner table.

The lady appeared to show no interest in me, but her coldness merely served to inflame my passions still further. I, of course, knew nothing of this virginal wife, and believed her coldness must derive from an excess of loyalty to her husband. And yet, she intrigued me. Had I not been mindful of my honour as a knight, and my reputation among my comrades in arms, I should without a doubt have made an attempt upon her honour that very night.

After we had eaten, her husband Sir Bercilak drew me aside and told me the woeful tale of his marriage. I could scarce believe that such a man as he – young and strong and vital – could accept such coldness from his bride and not merely force himself upon her and take what he would.'

'Alas, I cannot!' he replied. 'For it is not in my nature to be ungentle with a woman. I would that she would lie with me willingly; for if she will not therein lies no pleasure for me.'

'Then what are you to do, my lord?' I enquired of him. 'Are you resigned to live your life as a bachelor, with a comely virgin bride in this land of violence and darkness when any man might rob you of her at any moment?'

'Sir Gawain, I have heard tales of your conquests. You are a hot-blooded man, are you not?'

I knew not what to say, for in sooth I was afeared of sullying my reputation as an honourable and chivalric knight. And yet it was indeed true that I desired the wench, and I believed I was beginning to see the substance of his conversation. At length, I replied:

'A hot-blooded man, and yet an honourable one.'

'Then will you, good Sir Gawain, do me such a service as will gladden my heart and bind me still closer to the throne of Camelot, with ties of the deepest and most grateful obligation?'

I knew then that I could not refuse him. For in doing so, I should be going against the interests of my lord the King.

'If I may so do, and not sully my honour. Indeed, I shall perform whatever you request of me, Sir Bercilak.'

'Then I beg of you, use all the force of your will upon my wife Oruale, that she may become a complete and willing wife to me.'

I knew full well that he would have had me stop at persuasion and a little harmless flirtation. But I sensed in the depths of my black heart that, once alone with the Lady Oruale, my tastes for power over the female sex would surely overcome my better judgement, and lead me to acts of excess and indiscretion.

I said a courteous goodnight to my troubled host, and bid him cast all his anxieties from his mind. I would do my utmost to persuade his frosty wife to melt all her sweets upon him. But not, I thought to myself, until she had first melted them upon me.

I spent a restless night, troubled by the most indecent thoughts and dreams of my host's beautiful wife. I imagined her before me, utterly subjected to my will, begging of me mercy which I would not give. I would raise my hand to strike her and she would weep and beg me to spare her, crying out 'No, no more!' in the most piteous tones. But as the blow fell upon her naked upturned buttocks, she would cry out again, in joy and supplication: 'More, more, strike me again and yet again, my only master!'

My prick stiffened at the very thought of such pink and white nakedness before me, entirely at my disposal, reddening to crimson with each successive blow upon her twin delights. I began to stroke my shaft, toying lovingly with my stones and groaning with pleasure as I felt them grow heavy and ever-tauter in my greedy palm.

When at last a jet of pearly-white fluid burst forth from my loins, I almost believed that I was ejaculating over Oruale's rosy backside; and I came with a long, delicious groan of total pleasure.

The following morning, I discovered that Sir Bercilak had left early for a neighbouring manor, and would not be returning for three days. He had left instructions that I should take charge of his household – and his cold-hearted but delicious wife – during his absence.

Oruale was evidently much displeased by this arrangement, and was ill disposed to give me anything beyond the customary minimum of politeness. At breakfast, she sat and scowled at me, and made no secret of her displeasure. At length, I determined to force her into conversation.

'My Lady Oruale, what pleasures would you enjoy this fine day? For as you must know, your husband

Sir Bercilak has charged me with ensuring your complete satisfaction.'

She merely sat and glowered at me, her icy blue gaze striking shivers through me and making me even more determined to conquer her.

'Will you not answer me, my lady? For, since I have charge of you for these three days, do you not now owe me all the duties that a wife owes to her wedded husband?'

This had the desired effect of provoking her into fiery, icy life.

'Duties! I owe no duty to any man – and most assuredly not towards any man of the South Lands. For I am a free-born princess of the North Lands: a warrior-woman and noblewoman who would die rather than submit to such unworthy tyranny. You shall expect no "duties" from me, Sir Knight; for it is my husband who is your vassal, not I!'

'But lady, consider your position here at Orud-Ddur,' I continued with honeyed words, disguising the menace beneath. 'We are in wild lands, and a woman cast out into the forest would not long survive the depredations of wild animals – and worse. For the men of these lands are wild-eyed savages who enjoy their women as they enjoy their meat – they consume them until they are satiated, and then cast them away, broken and useless.'

'I fear no such fate.'

'Then you are more foolish than I thought, my lady. What could one lady do to protect herself in such a place? And, if you continue to displease me as you have displeased your husband, it may well be that I shall persuade him to cast you out to the wild men and leave you to suffer your fate.'

I knew, of course, that Sir Bercilak would do no

such thing; but I thought it would do no harm at all to remind the wench that she was but mortal flesh and very much dependent upon the goodwill of her menfolk for her survival. I looked at her and knew that my words had hit home; for her white skin had grown paler still, and she was gazing at me, wide-eyed but still defiant.

'This morn, you shall ride with me into the forest,' I decreed. And she knew that this was a command, and not a request.

We rode out alone, she on her white mare and I on a borrowed stallion from Sir Bercilak's stables: a strong-willed beast with a flashing eye, who sniffed the air and pawed the ground in his anxiety to reach the mare, which I soon realised was in season, a fact which I believed might well favour my plans.

After an hour the Lady Oruale – who had spent the entire ride in silence – pleaded fatigue, and asked if we might return to the castle. I laughed to myself, for I knew this was a ploy to return to the relative safety of the castle walls, where I might less easily threaten her honour.

'My dear lady,' I replied, 'if you are weary, then we shall rest awhile. See: there is a clearing just ahead, and we may rest ourselves by the river and refresh our appetites.'

With satisfaction, I noted the look of alarm in Oruale's ice-blue eyes. But she knew she must obey me, and rode her mare obediently into the clearing. Alas, she knew also that she would need my assistance to dismount; and it was with the greatest reluctance that she reached down to me and allowed me to take hold of her slender waist. As I lifted her down, I took the opportunity to slide my greedy hand up beneath her skirt. An immense thrill rippled through me as I made contact with her bare, smooth buttocks – for, in common with other Northwomen, she wore only rough linen shifts beneath her dress.

So! My lady had only her virtue to protect her! And to judge from the shivers and trembling of the wench beneath my fingers, she knew as well as I that she would need greater protection than that to save her from my determined purpose.

Nor was the lady as indifferent to my attentions as she pretended to be. For it was a long moment before she began to struggle in my arms and demand to be set down upon the ground. What's more, I had in passing contrived to run a hungry finger along the length of her cleft, and found its juiciness warm and welcoming. I would conquer her yet.

'Unhand me, Sir Knight!' cried the Lady Oruale. With a smile I set her on her feet, not before I had grasped a good handful of her arse-flesh and squeezed it hard enough to cause her pain. Pain which she seemed, perversely, to enjoy.

We sat down upon the grass, for it was a hot day and warm sunshine was filtering down through the trees. She gazed into the river and its reflected sparkle lit up her ice-blue eyes. The dappled sunlight played lightly across her bosom, for the dress she wore was tight-fitting and cut very low in the bodice. How I yearned to tear it from her body, to sink my teeth into that soft, warm flesh, to bite the rosy nipples which I knew lurked beneath the modest fabric of her white gown. How I longed to bespatter the clean, white woollen stuff with my abundant seed.

'See!' I cried. 'My horse knows his own mind and takes what he would have, without demur!'

She turned her head, and watched in wide-eyed, half-horrified fascination as my lusty stallion sniffed about the rear of her timid mare, and set about showing his interest in her in a most delightful and demonstrative way. His lively prick began to swell and grow to a most impressive length, and he reared on to his back legs and brought his forelegs down upon the unsettled mare's back, biting into her neck to prevent her from escaping him. Alas, though massively erect, his penis sought in vain to enter her, and he neighed piteously with frustration.

'The poor fellow needs assistance,' I remarked, slyly. 'And you shall assist him, my lady!'

'Whatever do you mean? To be sure, I shall do no such thing!' She started at me in amazement as she realised what I was bidding her to do. But, though she strained to pull away from my grasp, I had her fast by the wrist.

I led her over the rough, dusty ground to where the stallion and mare were still struggling in their embrace. And I prised her fingers open, though she resisted me, and placed the stallion's massive penis in her open palm. She shrieked with surprise to find her maiden's fingers holding so terrible a thing, but I noticed with great interest that her resistance was beginning to wane. There was a look of strange fascination in her eyes as she looked down at the immense erection in her hand, and she seemed paralysed between desire and dismay.

'Take the stallion's shaft and put him to the mare,' I commanded Oruale, greatly excited for my part to see this proud ice maiden's fingers clasped almost reverently about the horse's penis. My own member was swelling with eagerness within my hose, and I longed to throw the maiden down upon the grass and ravish her there and then, as the stallion was about to ravish the mare.

Seeing her sluggish, I placed my own hand upon Oruale's and began to guide the stallion's massive appendage towards its goal.

'I . . . I will not do this thing,' she mumbled, attempting to wrest her hand from my grasp. But in her heart of hearts she did not want to. For this demonstration of the intractable demands of nature had wakened within the maiden an intense curiosity to witness the act taking place.

'I shall do it with you,' I replied, and – my hand still upon hers – I took firm hold of the stallion's shaft and guided it to its target. With a neigh of pleasure, the stallion thrust home into the mare, and began to ride her joyously.

'Feel it, feel it,' I whispered into Oruale's ear, for her hand was still upon the horse's penis. 'That is how the stallion rides his mare, and how the man rides his lady. Would you not also like to ride?'

I prised her fingers free and led her a short distance away, for she seemed in a daze. I could see that the points of her breasts had hardened and were pressing against the fabric of her bodice. I knew that at that moment I might take her upon the grass and she would offer no resistance. But that would be too, too easy by far, and I had other plans for my Lady Oruale.

I let go of Oruale's wrist, and she sank to the ground, still panting, and rubbing the circulation back into her flesh. I did not let her rest long. Within moments, I had pulled her to her feet.

'Undress,' I ordered her.

'For no man!' she cried; and to my immense surprise, the wench pulled a little silver dagger out of her bodice and lunged at me with it, teeth bared and eyes flashing as she fought to preserve her honour.

But I was too swift for her. In a moment I had disarmed her and cast the silver blade to the fishes in the river. I held her about the waist, with her arms twisted behind her back.

I repeated my command: 'Undress. Now. Remember: I have absolute power over you. Power to hurt and harm. And I will, if you do not obey me now.'

With a look of purest hatred, the flaxen princess began to take off her clothes, there in the sun-dappled clearing. Her hands shook as she struggled with the laces which held her dress together at the back.

'I cannot,' she said, in a dull voice devoid of emotion. 'If you would have me naked, you needs must do the deed yourself.'

I needed no further encouragement, and set to the task with a worthy diligence. I fumbled with the laces, but found them intractable and they tried my patience so thoroughly that I unsheathed my sword, and with one swish of the blade, cut the laces from neck to waist. The princess stood stock still and did not flinch, though the blade touched her neck as it swept past.

The bodice fell from her shoulders, revealing a coarse linen shift beneath. I tugged at the dress and succeeded in pulling it down over Oruale's hips, letting it fall in pale folds about her feet. Then I turned the lady to face me.

'Step out of your dress,' I ordered. She obeyed. 'Now take off your shift. I want to see you completely naked.'

Slowly and mechanically, she bent down and seized the hem of her shift in both hands. Then she lifted it up – above her knees, her waist, and at last over her head, casting the discarded shift on to the ground.

She was indeed a fair sight: pale-skinned with a

rosey glow that belied her icy gaze. Her ample breasts stood out proudly, her stiff, pink nipples betraying the spring tide of desire which was rising within her youthful frame.

'Have you desires, Oruale?' I questioned her.

'I desire no man who is unworthy of me.'

'Do you desire me, Oruale?'

She glared at me contemptuously, but there was a faraway fire in her eyes as she spoke:

'I . . . How could I desire such as you? My blood is royal, and my body is for none save those of a royal house. And you cannot harm me. I am protected by the magic of a great white witch . . .'

'You are wrong, Oruale,' I hissed in her ear. 'Your body is for any man who desires it. And this day shall your body be my plaything, and the plaything of all who have desired you for so long. Magic will not save you now.'

With a cry of anger and distress, the Lady Oruale lifted her arms to the heavens and began to intone words in a strange language I could not understand. Words of power, of invocation. But none heard them save me, and I would show her no pity.

'Betrayed!' she cried. 'Abandoned and forlorn! Will you not be mindful of your honour, Sir Knight? Would you impose such base desires upon a high-born lady?'

I laughed, for in truth I was enjoying the sport. 'My Lady Oruale, your husband gave me charge of you. For these three days, you are mine to dispose of as I wish.'

The lady's nakedness was indeed lovely to behold. I longed to bury myself in that sweet flesh, where no man had ever laid his hand or thrust his prick. I longed to be her despoiler, to deflower her on the

43

greensward, and hear her piteous cries as I took my pleasure. But I have always had a fondness for a little piquancy in my lovemaking; and also it would not suffice merely to take the woman – I must also utterly break her spirit and make her well disposed to accept her husband's advances.

Before she realised what was happening, I had stripped the tack from her mare and was using it to bind my very own mount: Oruale would be my steed this day, and would bear my weight upon her loins.

I forced the woman to her knees and prised open her mouth, despite her protesting cries. And into it I pressed the horse's metal bit, binding the rest of the harness over her face, head and neck, so that the reins trailed down her back. Next, I pushed her forward so that she fell to hands and knees, like a handsome beast, her backside thrusting towards me as invitingly as any mare presenting herself to her stallion.

The saddle came next, the girth tightened about her slender waist so that the heavy leather would sit securely on her back. It was rough and cold, and must have weighed uncomfortably on her slender frame; but the bit in her mouth prevented her from crying out in protest.

And last of all came a wide leather band which I wound round between her thighs and backside like a crupper, forcing apart those creamy-white treasures, which she had guarded from sight for so long. How I delighted in the divine revelation of her sex, pink and moist and deliciously tight, and the puckered amber of her arsehole, no less inviting to my greedy eyes.

I moved around her, holding the reins by which I might control her movements, and inspecting my new steed. I was greatly excited to see that her dove-soft white breasts were now hanging down like delicious, juicy fruit waiting to be plucked from the tree. Although she tried desperately to clench her buttocks and hide her treasures from me, her arse-cheeks gaped defiantly wide and she no longer had any secrets from me.

With my dagger, I cut a hazel switch and flexed it between my fingers. It was supple and wiry. Then I half-sat, half-stood astride her (for my full weight would have crushed her frail body), and raised the switch to spur her on.

'Gee up!' I cried, and brought the hazel switch down upon the ice maiden's delightful rump. A muffled cry confirmed that my blow had hit home, but the princess stood her ground and refused to move.

I struck her again, harder this time, and commanded her.

'Move! Or it will be the worse for you, jade.'

This time, she obeyed, albeit reluctantly, moving hands and feet sluggishly forward across the grass.

'Once around the clearing, noble steed!' I was indeed enjoying the charade mightily. Sometimes she would stumble, and I would punish her for her clumsiness with another taste of the lash upon her juicy rump. She started, and tried to cry out, but I kept the bit locked firmly between her teeth.

Poor Oruale! Her backside was soon marbled red and white, and I could hear her breathing quickening and growing more shallow. This pleased me greatly, for I knew it to be a sign of her weakening resistance. In spite of herself, the ice princess was beginning to derive pleasure from my mastery of her body.

At length, I grew weary of our slow promenade around the clearing; and I swung round so that I was facing my steed's swelling rump. The flexible tip of the slender hazel switch was an ideal instrument, and I swiftly set about using it to titillate the delicate tissues around her arsehole. Oh! how she writhed and twisted about under these delicious tortures, especially when I pressed the tip of the switch against the puckered nether mouth and gave it a gentle thrust, sending it into the depths of her with no more difficulty than one might have in pressing a knife into butter.

I amused myself for a while, twisting and turning the hazel-switch in Oruale's arse, and using it to widen the passage a little. For she would need space to welcome another guest before the day was over.

Taking the hazel switch from her arse, I leant a little further forward and inspected the rosy glories of my lady's virgin womanhood. Oh, the delight of seeing such chaste tightness, growing so wet and willing. I knew now that my Lady Oruale was on the very brink of submission. I must not flinch now from my noble purpose.

And, still astride my exotic steed, I began to stroke Oruale's outer lips, teasing the bright blonde curls which framed her maiden modesty. I was rewarded with a series of low moans, and noted with suspicion that, in spite of her high-minded resolutions, my lady was growing ever wetter under my touch.

I slid my finger nearer to the virgin hole, excited beyond belief by the slippery touch of her juices on my fingertip. My manhood was straining against the fabric of my hose, and I knew that I had only to pull it out and leap upon Oruale's proffered rump to satisfy my every physical urge. But I wanted more.

At last, I slid my finger inside the tight, wet orifice, the better to explore its uncharted glories. Barely half of my finger was inside her before she winced and I realised that I had come up against my Lady Oruale's maidenhead. So it was indeed true that she was still a virgin bride, these many months since her wedding night! I pressed again against the membrane and found it thick and taut. Her defloration would not be an easy task.

I now climbed off the lady, and unfastened the girth which held the saddle on her back. I helped her to her feet, for she was stiff and shaky from her ordeal and inspected her. She was the fairest of all sights I have seen: entirely naked save for the bit and harness about her head and shoulders, and the crupper, drawn between her luscious thighs, which forced her to stand with her legs a little apart, her sex and arse still on display for all the world to see. Her long, pink nipples were fully erect and formed the stalks to the most appetising fruit I had ever seen. How I longed to sink my teeth into those creamy-white globes, and then taste the lady's juices, to feel them flooding over my parched and greedy tongue.

Taking hold of her wrist once again, I half-led, half-dragged her to her own mare, who had now recovered her composure after her recent amorous exploits, and was peacefully munching grass.

The Lady Oruale cast me a glance of fear as I produced some more leather straps from my panniers: I had come well prepared for this little mystery play which we were acting out.

I took four of the longest leather straps and, buckling them together in the middle to form two long straps, slung them over the mare's saddle, so that they hung down on either side. Then I made Oruale lie down on the ground, face down, beneath

47

the mare's belly. I then attached the ends of the straps about her ankles and wrists. By means of tightening the buckles in the middle of the straps I was able gradually to raise her helpless body off the ground, until at last she was swaying, face down, starfish-like, at about waist height. I then took the reins about her neck and tied them to the saddle, so that her head was supported and facing forwards.

Oruale hung beneath the mare's belly, silent and still: her legs forced wide apart by the leather straps, and her delicious breasts pendulous and trembling. There was a look of terror in her eyes, for she knew herself utterly helpless and at the mercy of whatever whim I should choose to inflict upon her. And there was another look in her eyes also: a look of newly awakening lust, of repressed womanhood which begs to be released from its prison.

I knelt beneath her and began to explore the flesh which now lay so beautifully open to my attentions. She had a perfect body: the body of a snow queen whose iciness conceals a cold but ferocious flame within.

I began with her breasts, for they had tormented me from the first, with their rounded perfection, their downy softness crested with the pink hardness of her erect nipples. I stroked them, kneaded them, felt their weight in my hands. They were soft and mobile, and invited me to kiss and lick and suck them. I took one nipple in my mouth and began to nibble at it gently, whilst pinching the other between finger and thumb. My Lady Oruale's breathing became yet quicker and more hoarse, and a low moaning issued forth from her gagged mouth.

When I had enjoyed these delights to the full, I moved my attention to her lips. They were rosy and full, and many times I had pictured them closing upon my eager manhood, drinking its plenty and supping at its spring. I inserted a finger between her lips and removed the bit.

'Untie me and let me go free, tyrant! You are an unworthy and licentious knave, no knight!' she cried in fury, eager still to play the wronged virgin – yet I saw still the look of burning lust in her eyes. She made as though to bite my finger, and I scolded her:

'Bite and you shall feel worse than my hazel switch on your backside, impudent hussy! Do as I bid you, or you shall be thrown to the wolves and the masterless men who roam these forests!'

And without further ado, I took down the front of my hose and pulled out my manhood, more eager than ever for the fray. I placed its tip against her lips, and though the lady tried hard to close them against me, I quickly succeeded in ramming my weapon home, so far that it near choked her. But she did not try to hurt me, and on the contrary, began to suck at my hardness with an instinctive skill and enjoyment. Alas, so aroused was I and so silken soft the touch of Oruale's mouth upon my member that all too soon I was at my crisis, pouring my seed in a great hot tide down Oruale's throat. She tried to spit it out, but I refused to let her:

'Swallow it down, my lady,' I hissed. 'It is the essence of life, your baptism to fleshly lusts.' And she obeyed.

I withdrew from her mouth, leaving her gasping and weak. But the light of lust still sparkled in her eyes, and I knew that I had won the battle.

'And now for your baptism to womanhood,' I decreed.

I knelt behind her, with my face on a level with her ever-moistening opening, and began to lap at her wetness. She began to groan with pleasure as my tongue searched out the hard nubbin of her clitoris and licked it, at first slowly and gently, and then harder and more furiously.

'Ah, ah . . . Yes!' she cried, as she felt her first-ever crisis approaching. And I, chivalrous knight that I am, could not refuse her. I licked at her until at last she burst forth in a tide of fragrant love-juice and a cry of sudden unexpected ecstasy.

Before she had had a chance to come to her senses, I determined to conquer her last bastion of resistance. I saw with satisfaction that my soldier was once again well armed and ready for combat, and I placed his helmeted head against the well-oiled entrance, grasping her thighs to gain a better purchase.

My first attempts at entering her ended in cries of anguish from my Lady Oruale, for her maidenhead was tough and unyielding. But a second determined assault gained me entrance to her secret places. I felt the membrane tearing as my member forced its eager way through the gates of her secret pleasure garden. How she cried out, and twisted and turned in her bonds, in a vain attempt to escape my all-conquering lance.

'No, no, you cannot!' she cried.

It was too late, for I had already stormed her battlements, and was at that very moment battering down the door to her castle keep.

I thrust into her hungrily. Her tunnel was soft and smooth and hot about my starving prick, and I knew that I should not be long within her. Already I could feel the seed gathering at the base of my shaft, ready to fountain forth into Oruale's wet cave.

'Yes, yes, it is happening again!'

Oruale was reaching her first crisis as a real woman, and I was more than happy to join in her pleasure, crying out as the seed sprang forth from my loins, and gushed into her belly.

I withdrew from her and saw with immense satisfaction that a river of mingled blood and seed was gushing out of her. The ice maiden was beginning to melt. But I had not finished with her yet. There was yet one more virgin pathway to conquer.

I began to toy once again with Oruale's arsehole, though she begged and pleaded with me to leave her that last shred of her modesty and dignity. What cared I for either? She was my plaything now, and the instrument and receptacle of my pleasure. Besides which, she seemed to be experiencing not a little pleasure herself.

Oruale's amber rose was tight, and dry. So I scooped up a little of her juices, and smeared them over the puckered nether mouth. She winced a little as I thrust first one, then two fingers into her forbidden place. But she did not forbid me. For I knew that she desired this as much as I did.

Three fingers now, and I judged her ready to receive my third tribute of the day. My manhood was erect and eager once again, and throbbing with excitement to see vagina and anus so immodestly displayed, forced apart by the leather straps of a horse's tack.

Without more ado, I seized her still-red buttocks and thrust into her. She cried out as I entered her, but then began to moan gently as I struck up a slow and leisurely rhythm, taking care to ensure her pleasure by toying all the while with her clitoris.

Her arse was gloriously tight and held me fast as

a tight fist about my penis. With my hands around her thighs, I pulled in and out of her with ever-harder thrusts, until at last we came together in a great cry of desire and fulfilment.

When I untied the Lady Oruale, she was in a swoon from which she did not wake until we reached Castle Orud-Ddur and she was put to bed. I had taken care to disorder my dress also, and to inflict upon myself a small wound upon my sword arm – for we had been, so I related, ambushed by masterless men from the marcher lands who had captured the Lady Oruale when she foolishly ran away from me. It had only been through great personal danger that I had at last succeeded in rescuing her, alas ravished but otherwise unharmed.

The Lady Oruale made no attempt to contradict my story. Indeed, I spent the next two nights in Oruale's bed, teaching her the ways of womanhood.

On the third day, when Sir Bercilak returned, his castle was in good order and his wife restored to health, with a new sparkle in her ice-blue eyes. When she greeted him, she took him to her bedchamber and nothing more was seen of either of them for several days.

Sir Kay

*T*he veiled head was shaking with laughter.

'Sweet Sir Gawain,' cried the naked temptress, 'such chivalry demands a just reward! And since you bestowed such delights upon the Lady Oruale, is it not fitting that you too should sample their unique piquancy?'

'I . . . I do not understand,' blustered Gawain, his mind still reeling from the brutal suddenness with which he had found himself compelled to speak only the truth. 'What manner of words do you speak?'

'I speak of your reward, my fine young knight, who hath such fine, strong limbs and an impudent prick.'

'My reward . . .?'

Her black-swathed face gave no clue as to her meaning. But Gawain gazed dumbly upon the celestial, infernal, damnable beauty of her naked flesh and saw her nipples hardening with a secret excitement. And fear began to wrap itself about his heart as though it were the sorceress's dark and starry cloak.

'How interesting it would be – would it not? – to

toy with those limbs, that prick; and to see how pleasant it felt for you to have those limbs and that prick restrained and powerless. Say, Sir Gawain: is that not a good jest, a fine gift? Your reward, good Sir Knight, is to taste those special delights with which you paid your homage to the Lady Oruale. Therefore taste the sweetness of humility.'

Bending to pick up her staff, the sorceress tapped it three times upon the table, striking a shower of golden sparks from its silver tip. Then she raised it to shoulder height and pointed it towards Gawain, intoning the incantation:

'Amene, Amene, Takiel.'

At once, Sir Gawain felt fierce bonds fasten about his arms and legs, forbidding all movement. He looked down in panic, hoping to reach for his dagger and cut through the thongs that held him fast in his chair. But there was nothing there. The power of sorcery held him as surely as any iron bands or leather thongs.

And as he watched, the veiled sorceress leant over his shoulder and unfastened the cord holding his hose about his waist. She pulled down the top of his hose and exposed his prick, grunting appreciatively as it grew longer and hotter and stiffer between her cool white fingers. Was she then going to gratify him? Was that to be his reward? Was she about to relieve this terrible rising tide of frustration with hands and lips and tongue? Was she going to straddle his thighs and take his manhood into her soft moistness? He sighed with extreme pleasure as her caresses brought him to a fever pitch of desire.

'Now, now, now!' he moaned, completely oblivious now to his fellow knights and his King, seated around the table and already amazed and horrified by what had come forth from his lips. 'Fuck me, suck me . . . Anything!'

The sorceress threw back her head and laughed, her big soft breasts trembling with each silvery peal of mirth.

'Alas no, good Sir Knight.'

She removed her fingers from his massively swollen prick, letting it spring back, taut and yearning, against his belly.

Gawain gazed at her in horror. 'Surely . . . You cannot leave me like this: helpless and with my manhood yearning for you!'

'Accept your reward, Sir Gawain. And accept it in patient silence, for we have many other tales to hear tonight; there are many other knights as ready as you to tell their tales and vie for the honour of my bed and body, for the honour of becoming my slave.

'Therefore, join your brother knight in sweet servitude!'

Arthur raised his hand to the pommel of his trusty broadsword Excalibur; but it was a vain attempt. As he touched it, the hilt grew white hot and seared his fingers with an incandescence which drew a great cry of agony forth from his lips.

'Will you not learn, Sire, that you cannot strike at me? That I am protected by magic – the magic which your own Master Merlin has bestowed upon me so generously throughout the days and nights of our joining.

'Strike against me, and you are striking against yourselves, my lords. Resist me, and you will perish. Humour me, satisfy my whims and desires, and you shall perhaps share in my immortality.'

The sorceress turned to the knight seated on the right of Sir Gawain: a tall blond youth with grey eyes and full, sensual lips.

'Have you a tale to tell us, Sir Kay?'

The youth looked up from the table, his eyes flashing with anger, and defiance in the pout of his lips.

'I shall tell you nought, for I have nought to tell.'

The sorceress stood behind him now, and he could feel the soft, warm cloud of her breath on the back of his neck, coaxing the short blond hairs to attention – mirroring the upward thrust of his mercilessly enthusiastic young cock, which was indeed preparing to crow forth its defiance.

'Fie, Sir Kay! You cannot lie to me. Such a fine youth as you must have enjoyed many a serving wench, many a country slut.'

At this implication, the young knight's fury bubbled to the surface and he cried out in anger: 'I am a knight of the Round Table, a servant of none save the King. And I am of noble blood, and would have no congress with serving wenches and farm girls. For I am vowed to beauty and gentility, to refinement and courtly love.'

'Ah!' cried the sorceress. 'So your taste is not for lowly serving wenches, but for their noble mistresses? Speak truth, Sir Kay: tell forth the tale of your most heroic exploit with the fair sex. Was there not a lady of the Northern Kingdoms – a Lady Gisela? Did you not play some pretty music upon that sweetest of instruments?'

Sir Kay opened his mouth to deny everything the sorceress had charged him with, but – oh horror! – no sooner had he parted his lips than words of the most ignominious truth came spilling forth.

THE TALE OF SIR KAY
AND THE LADY GISELA

It was a year ago, in the early summer, and I was then only newly a knight – for I had been a poor squire, in the service of other knights, since my thirteenth summer.

I came of a poor family; my father was a yeoman farmer, and my mother had been a maid-in-waiting to the Lady Guinevere before her marriage. It was through my mother's agency that I was granted admittance to the court of Camelot, there to learn knightly skills and courtly arts, and to perfect my understanding of the chivalric code. Upon the sixteenth anniversary of my birth, I underwent the prescribed ordeals and was dubbed a Knight of the Round Table.

I was greatly puffed up with pride in my new knightliness, for I had long coveted the arms and banneret of a Knight of the Round Table. I craved a chance to prove myself a worthy knight; and when Merlin called me to him and charged me with an errand of the highest importance, I was eager to sally forth upon the King's business. My masters and my comrades believed in the purity of my heart and the goodness of my intent, though in the depths of my heart I was lustful and proud, hungry for self-aggrandisement and for the taste of sweet and noble flesh.

I rode out the following morning, bound for the Northern Kingdoms, there to deliver a most important gift, sent from Merlin to Prince Aelfrith, the elderly ruler of a northern princedom who had decided, in the twilight of his years, to take a young wife to bear him an heir to his inheritance.

Alas, Prince Aelfrith was growing old, and as his

eyes dimmed so did the flame of his potency. Afraid that he would not have strength enough to take his bride on her wedding night, he sent messengers to his good friend Merlin, entreating him to send magical powders and amulets which would bestir his cock and a love charm to render him handsome and desirable in the eyes of his toothsome young bride. These Merlin duly prepared and entrusted to my care, for he believed me an honourable young man, eager to prove my trustworthiness as a knight.

Sad to tell, I had already half-formed a plan which would have brought disgrace upon me, and upon the name of Camelot, had anyone but myself been aware of it.

It took me a week to ride north to the castle of Prince Aelfrith, which loomed dark and massive above thickly wooded hills. I was greeted by a comely maid who directed me to my apartments.

'The Prince is out hunting today,' she told me, simpering a little, for I could tell she found my person agreeable – and in truth, though such a common little slut as she was scarcely meat enough for me, I felt my youthful exuberance rising inside my hose and began to tell myself, indeed, there were worse ways to pass the time.

'He will not be back before three days, good Sir Knight,' went on the lass, her two tanned bubbies wobbling deliciously within their skimpy prison – for she wore the lowest-cut bodice that decency would allow, barely covering the deep pink tips of her breasts, which nevertheless poked their impudent little noses through the clinging fabric of her light summer gown. 'This night you dine with the Lady Gisela, the prince's bride-to-be. You are to be her honoured guest. In the meantime, is there ought that I can do to please or amuse you, master?'

I am not an unobservant fellow; nor was I indifferent to the way she had unfastened the top button of her gown, the better to let me see down into the deep, succulent cleft between those two tight-squeezed breasts. It pleased me greatly that she flattered me with the title of 'good Sir Knight', and 'master'. Aye, in truth, I had a yen to play the master with this little country slattern.

'Go over to the door and lock it,' I commanded her. At once, a broad smile of understanding passed across her honest country face, and her pretty blonde waves bobbed up and down on her bare shoulders as she hurried to the door and turned the heavy iron key deftly in the lock.

'Now come to me,' I ordered her.

'Yes, master.' She obeyed, and – to my surprise and pleasure – knelt down before me with the utmost reverence and began to toy with my most privy parts through the fabric of my hose.

'No: not yet,' I scolded her, in mock indignation. 'Not until I give you the command. Only then may you touch the fleshly lance.'

'Then I must be punished, master,' she breathed, playing the little penitent to perfection, her eyes downcast but her titties thrust well forward to give me the full benefit of their rounded splendours.

Ah yes – a punishment, indeed. But what punishment should I impose? Something irksome, something a little uncomfortable, undoubtedly. But nothing to dampen her ardour, for after punishment would come pleasure.

'Bend forward, over the chair,' I commanded her.

She did so, and I hoisted up her skirt and cotton

shift above her waist, bunching them and knotting them up so that she was naked from the waist down, bare-buttocked and bare-legged, her feet clad only in rough open sandals.

I inspected her as meticulously as a general inspecting his troops. Her skin was a pale nut brown, downy like a peach; and I knew that she must have spent many hours gambolling naked in the spring sunshine to have such a beautiful tanned body.

'Your skin is very tanned,' I remarked. 'Even the skin of your backside is a tawny brown. Where is your modesty, little slut?'

She gave a suppressed little giggle as the palm of my hand explored these sun-blessed realms.

'The Prince likes the serving women to go naked in the summer,' she explained. 'He says it reminds him of summer days when he was young, and that it awakens his manhood.'

'And so, have you awakened his lust? Has the Prince enjoyed you?'

'Gramercy, no, sir! But he likes for to see me suck the cocks of the village lads, and he gives me a penny if I'll fuck with Old Tom, and let him watch. Old Tom, he be the cellarer here. Very old he is, but he has such a great big dick you'd hardly believe it! Fucks like a stallion, he does.'

I was beginning to feel rather like a stallion myself by now: hard and smooth and taut-bollocked. I imagined myself with a massive stallion's erection, mighty and fearsome, forcing myself between the tawny buttocks before me and into the belly of this shameless young hussy. Not the noble girl I had hoped for, but good sport, I doubted not.

'Such filthy talk, and from the mouth of a young maiden!' I cried in mock disgust, suppressing a smile as I spoke the word 'maiden', for I doubted not it had been many a long year since her maidenhead had been offered to Old Tom or some other village ruffian. 'Now, brace yourself against the wall, for I intend to give you a well-deserved whipping!'

Leaning over the chairback, the girl placed her palms flat against the wall and braced herself for the onslaught. I could restrain myself no longer, for she was thrusting her broad, fleshy backside out at me and my hand itched to strike her.

I seized my sword in both hands, and turned it round so that the flat of the blade was angled towards my buttocks. With a heave I swung it and brought it whistling down upon the waiting flesh. She gave a great howl as the cold metal whacked against her backside. But, much to my satisfaction, she began to shuffle her feet apart and to open her thighs, as though begging me for ever-harsher punishment. How could I refuse her?

And I brought the flat of the sword down again and again upon those glowing golden buttocks, which were soon radiant with a far hotter fire. Each successive blow brought her thighs further apart, and she began to make a low growling sound like a she-wolf on heat, urging her mate to bite into her slender throat and enter her savagely with his throbbing prick.

'Wicked, wicked girl!' I panted as I chastised her with my trusty blade.

'Aye, wicked, my lord,' she gasped, relishing the cold steel as it slapped down again and again on these wonderful, fleshy arse-cheeks. They were reddening like juicy fruits ripening in the sunshine, and I imagined my teeth sinking into their flesh.

Casting aside my sword, I pulled down the front

of my hose and released my straining prick, which reared its fine purple head as nobly and as willingly as any thoroughbred: a fine warhorse indeed, ready to do battle, and well armoured in its glistening helmet, its shaft hardened and girded for the fray.

I grabbed hold of the little hussy's arse-cheeks and shivered with pleasure at her little squeal of surprise as I gripped them firmly and squeezed, glorifying in their firm juiciness. Still gripping them tightly, I forced them apart like the two halves of a ripe peach, the better to enjoy the glories within. Ah, this was indeed a ripe peach, for its heart oozed juice, as fragrant and sweet as any I have ever tasted. I ran my finger greedily down the girl's sopping crack and savoured the juice upon my tongue. It was sweet and rich, with a musky aftertaste, and the explosion of its scents within my mouth inflamed me so greatly that I could hold back no longer.

'Punish me, my lord!' she cried, thrusting her backside towards me in a lewd parody of penance. 'Run me through!'

Tormenting her little brown bumhole for a while, I soon had her moaning and writhing beneath my touch, and her cunny-hole was streaming juice down her inviting brown thighs. I could restrain myself no more, and, taking firm hold of my swollen prick, I forced it into her proffered crack, joining her in a great sigh of pleasure as I felt its silken lips close about my member in a clinging embrace.

I rode her from need, rather than from passion. She was a little wild mare, delightful to dally with but of no consequence. It amused me to play her as one might play a folk instrument, producing a crude but exciting music with its own hot and insistent rhythms.

As I ploughed her furrow, I slipped my hand round to the front of her and fumbled roughly with the strings of her bodice, at last finding the knack and, with a swift pull, unlacing her dress so that her twin bubbies came tumbling out into my eager hands. They were fine and soft and warm, heavy and lively in my palms. I squeezed them and began to pinch the nipples, and was soon gratified by an undeniable stiffness. As they grew ever harder, ever larger, I felt a corresponding wetness spreading through the girl's nether parts, anointing my cock with a copious stream of love-dew.

The excitement of the ride soon told upon me, for it was many weeks since I had had a woman; and with regret it was over far too soon. She began to pant and writhe, and I felt her cunny-rings tightening as a her spasm approached. This delightful sensation communicated itself to my cock, and I spent instantly.

When I withdrew and took a few steps back from her, I saw that her thighs were running with floods of mingled spunk and love-juice – a sight so gratifying that my cock very nearly rose to attention on the instant.

The girl unfastened the folds of her skirt and let it fall decorously around her legs. I felt a sudden pang of regret as her beautiful strong thighs disappeared from view, but told myself that after all she was but a village strumpet, and that there would undoubtedly be much more important prey for me to stalk that night.

The plan had been half formed in my mind ever since I heard that Prince Aelfrith was an elderly man, often absent from his domain – as indeed he was this very day, the day of my arrival with his long-awaited wedding gifts from Merlin.

During the journey I had examined the packages I was carrying, though I had been warned not to pry into their contents. But I had oveheard Merlin telling his assistant what the packages contained, and in my youthful pride I told myself that his warnings need not apply to me. I opened the two packages, securely wrapped in deerskin, and found two bottles within. One contained a whitish, odourless powder, which was Merlin's recipe for male virility: his gift to ensure that his friend Aelfrith would never disappoint his bride or be incapable of begetting a lusty male heir. I saw from the label that only a few grains of the powder need be taken in order for it to take full and long-lasting effect. I told myself that surely the Prince would never miss a tiny spoonful . . . Stealthily, I transferred a spoonful to a twist of paper and placed it in my saddle-bag.

The other bottle contained a clear, pale pink syrup, which smelt faintly of rosewater. According to the label, this was an infallible love philtre, and just one small spoonful, administered to the subject, would ensure his or her complete devotion and desire for a period of twenty-four hours, after which the dose must be repeated.

A thought leapt unbidden in my mind. The Lady Gisela was a renowned beauty, but also known far and wide for her chastity, with not a stain upon her pure reputation since the death of her husband two years ago, when she was but a lass of sixteen and not long wed. Moreover, this morsel of delight was at this very moment resident in her future husband's castle, preparing for her wedding; and had she not bidden me to be her honoured guest at her private table this very evening?

Surely Gisela knew nothing of the measures which

her future husband had taken to ensure the success of their nuptial conjugation. She would be completely innocent of any real reason for being here in the castle at this time. No doubt she would assume that I had come only as an emissary from King Arthur, to attend her wedding (as indeed I had). Therefore she would suspect nothing, should I attempt a small experiment on my own account. After all, I must ensure that my master Merlin's gifts were indeed efficacious, must I not? Trembling with excited anticipation, I emptied out my water-flask and transferred a little of the liquid into it.

That evening, I was called by the same serving maid to attend my Lady Gisela for the evening meal. As luck would have it, she and I were the only guests in the castle, and – since she was a lady of spotless virtue and I an unimpeachable Knight of the Round Table – she had deemed it quite seemly that we should dine together, and alone. Which, of course, suited my plans admirably well.

I had bathed and dressed in my finest clothes: a red doublet edged in gold thread and black hose, with matching red and gold velvet slippers. These had been a gift from Queen Guinevere to mark my coming into the court of King Arthur, and I prided myself that I cut a pretty figure in them. Of course, if all went to plan it would not matter what I looked like.

I was ushered through the main dining hall of the castle, and into a small side-chamber, richly furnished and lit by dozens of candles, which illuminated the embroidered tapestries lining the thick stone walls. At the end of a long wooden table sat the most beautiful and exciting woman I have ever seen: aristocratic, slender, but with wonderfully swelling breasts which thrust their tips adventurously through the luxuriant cascade of her long chestnut hair. As she stood to greet me, I saw that she was tall and had a tiny waist, emphasised by her silver girdle and by the generous curve of her womanly hips.

She held out her hand to me and I knelt to kiss it, breathing in the mingled scent of roses and of her glorious womanhood, so near that I could have reached out and, lifting up the hem of her green velvet gown, bury my face in the glossy chestnut bush between her thighs. I looked up into her emerald green eyes, and longed to thrust my prick between her full red lips, make her suck at me, make this chaste, aristocratic beauty choke on the gift of my proud loins. I pictured her gagging on the flood tide of my seed, little trails of semen running out of the corners of her mouth; and I knew that I must have her.

I stood behind her chair and helped her chivalrously into her seat. Little did she suspect that, as she was sitting down, I was preoccupied with a far less noble pursuit: spilling a few drops of the love philtre into my lady's goblet, watching with glee as the pale pink liquid mingled with the dark red wine within.

I sat down in my own chair, and watched nervously as my Lady Gisela's hand strayed to the goblet and then away again, to her lap. Would she perhaps decide not to drink her wine? Would she suspect that it had been adulterated in some way? Had she seen what I had done? And if she did indeed drink down the love philtre, would it have the desired effect?

The food was very fine and delicious, yet it almost choked me to eat, for I was suffering agonies of doubt and suspense. I watched the lady's pretty lips toying with a morsel of bread, a berry, a sliver of roast swan, and dreamed that they were toying with my cock, my balls, my arse. I saw her bosom trembling as she laughed, or bent to cut her food. I saw the way her arm pushed against the side of her breast and made it swell and bulge as she cut the food with her knife, and I felt my manhood swelling and bulging in sympathy, straining for blessed release. As she shifted position on her chair, I imagined her beautiful backside squashing against the polished wood; the delicious arse-cheeks spreading, opening, pressing the amber rose of her little puckered arsehole against the fabric of her shift, her tight-fitting velvet gown.

I must have her, I thought.

At last, at last; Gisela choked on a piece of bread and began to cough.

'Perhaps a draught of wine, madam?' I heard myself suggesting, in a surprisingly confident voice.

'Yes . . . perhaps you are right.' Still coughing a little, Gisela picked up her goblet and took a few sips. The coughing subsided, and I feared she might drink no more, but I need not have worried, for she raised it once again to her luscious lips and drained it in a single draught.

Now, all I had to do was wait.

To my amazement, a change began to steal over the Lady Gisela almost immediately. Her eyes seemed to grow brighter and she turned her gaze on me, seeming to fix me with a growing fascination. In the silence of the dining hall, I could distinctly hear her breathing quickening and becoming heavier.

She turned to the wench who was serving us: 'You may leave us. Go now.'

The girl curtsied and left the room, pulling the heavy brocade curtain across the doorway as she went. I was alone at last with Gisela, her green eyes sparkling in the flickering candlelight, her soft, ample bosom quivering as she held out her arms to me:

'My lord,' she whispered. 'My only desire . . .'

'Gisela!' I could hardly believe my good fortune. Fumbling in the leather pouch slung about my waist, I reached for the paper twist and – although in my present turgid state I hardly thought I needed it – sprinkled a pinch of the white powder into my own wine, which I drank down in one gulp.

Within seconds, I felt myself transported to another plane – a plane of infinitely higher ecstasy, where desire reached such a peak as I had never before known, never even dreamed of. My youthful body, ever lustful, ever eager, felt as though it had been magnified a thousand times, its every nerve stretched to breaking point with the need and the want and the violence of my passion.

I reached down for my prick and felt it through the fabric of my hose. It felt like an alien being, a presence that was and yet was not of my body, an engine of massive power and energy; a serpent uncoiling and waiting to strike, to dart forward and spit out its venom.

'What is your desire, my lord?' breathed Gisela: an utterly changed woman from the quietly spoken, reserved, almost virginal widow who had welcomed me to her table with downcast eyes and words of cool politeness, utterly devoid of the base desires which now animated her every look, her every word, her every movement, her every breath. 'Tell me what it is you would have me do.'

'Then tell me this, my lady: do you desire me, Gisela?'

'I desire you with every fibre of my being, my lord.'

'Tell me of your desire. I want to hear every word, every thought translated into speech and deed.'

'I desire you with all that there is in me. My womanhood, that has lain empty for so long, gapes wide and aches with emptiness for it yearns for you to fill it to overflowing. My breasts ache for the touch of your fingers, your lips, your teeth. Let me suckle you as I would suckle a tiny babe, my lord; and all the while you are drawing milk from my dugs, I shall be drawing forth your seed from your loins with my thighs and fingers and mouth. And there is another secret place . . . I dare not say.'

'Tell it to me, if you wish me to fulfil your desires.'

'It is my arse. It also aches for you, my lord. I gaze at you and see that you are comely, and my arse cries out for your touch, your kiss, your thrust. What do you desire of me now, my lord?'

I was overcome with elation and desire. The fiery warmth in my groin seemed to be spreading through my entire body, and the urgency was terrible to feel. I knew that the powder I had taken would sustain me through many triumphs, many orgasms, and yet I was loth to give in to my desire so quickly, without first tormenting it – and the lady – a little, the better to enjoy the conquest of both.

I smiled to myself. 'I desire that you disrobe for me: here, now, in this room; and that you come to me and do my will.'

A troubled look passed across her face.

'But what if we should be discovered? There are guards and servants all around. Only a curtain separates us from the main hall of the castle. What if someone should enter and find us here?'

'Do you not desire me, Gisela? Do you not feel already the touch of my tongue on your clitty, my prick in your sex, my finger stretching the skin of your arse?'

'I desire you.'

'Then you will do as I desire.'

At that moment the love philtre seemed to complete its work, for the shadow passed from her face and Gisela became the most complete, the most obedient, the most aristocratic, and the most satisfying slave a man could desire.

First of all, she unfastened the silver girdle about her waist. It was in the form of a serpent, with its tail in its mouth; and it set my mind to feverish images of my own lively serpent, burying its head in the warmth and wetness between the Lady Gisela's thighs. She placed the girdle on the table, and then reached behind her to fumble with the laces which held the tight velvet gown in place.

After a few moments, she succeeded in unfastening the gown and, reaching up, she pulled the bodice down off her shoulders, until it rested on her hips, revealing more of her beautiful breasts, clad only in an embroidered linen shift which emphasised the stiffening points of her love-hungry nipples.

She then took hold of the dress and, pulling the tight fabric down over her hips, not without a little difficulty, stepped out of the dress and laid it over the back of her chair.

She stood bare-armed before me in her shift: dressed as only her maid-in-waiting had seen her for the last two years, since the death of her new husband in battle. And perhaps even he had seldom seen her so open, so bare, so willing; for she was a virtuous and modest lady indeed. Until this night.

The shift was fastened up the front with a series of small bows. These yielded easily to her fingers, and the sides of the shift parted to reveal the most divine nakedness underneath. I gasped at her loveliness, at the expanse of faultless white flesh which none had seen or touched for so long; and I hungered for her with all of my being.

Gisela cast off the shift and walked towards me, a smile of the most extreme, the most overwhelming desire spreading across her face. I knew then that she was utterly at the mercy of the love philtre – and of myself.

She stood before me, obedient yet restless: eager for the command which would free her from the last restraints of modesty and permit her to unleash the full onslaught of her long-repressed desires upon my body. I took pity on her in her distress.

'Gisela, you may undress me and suck me off.'

With a moan of joy, the Lady Gisela threw herself upon me and began to pull off my clothes. I had to restrain her a little, lest she damage my costly clothes, the only good ones I possessed. But she soon had me as naked as she, whereupon she fell to her knees and began pawing and licking at my prick and balls, which tensed up with delight instantly, and threatened to shoot their load before she had even taken my manhood into her wonderful full-lipped mouth.

Eager to enjoy her, I pulled Gisela's head down towards my groin and opened her mouth wide with my fingers, pushing my stiff manhood into her mouth. I gave a great cry of joy as I felt her warm, moist tongue slide across the smooth dome of my hardened shaft; and I pulled her closer to me, so that my cock could slide further down her grateful throat.

She sucked and licked me eagerly, hungrily; and as with one hand I set the rhythm of her lips, with the other I urged her on to her own peaks of pleasure, pinching and rolling her hardened nipples between finger and thumb.

All too soon, I felt the seed building up at the base of my shaft, and with a gasp of ecstasy – for I dared not shout out my joy – I thrust harder than ever into the girl's throat, bursting forth in torrents which near choked the poor woman, who fell coughing at my feet, the semen still trailing from her full red lips. I drew her to her feet and kissed her passionately, savouring the salty taste of my own seed.

And it was as though the taste itself revived me, or activated the power of the white powder I had swallowed; for no sooner had I finished spending my seed, than my cock reared its head proudly once again, even more painfully erect than before, and bursting anew with the abundant gift of my semen. Even in my youthfulness, I had never before experienced such amazing powers of recovery, and I blessed the potion which allowed me such unfailing potency.

Gisela gazed into my eyes, and I felt her fingers exploring my shaft once again, evidently approving of its renewed stiffness. She was evidently in desperate need of relief herself, for she began to moan and, parting her thighs, she rubbed her downy mound against my leg as though trying to bring herself off.

I pushed her away, for I wanted to be the agent of her pleasure. She whimpered at such cruel treatment, but soon began to moan with pleasure once again when I inserted an exploratory finger into her. She was dripping with wetness, yet very tight – for this young woman was almost a virgin still, her husband had but few chances to enjoy her before his untimely death on the field of battle.

I scooped up some of the abundant juices, and used

them to lubricate the throbbing button I discovered towards the front of her body. She began to clutch at me, tighter and tighter, and to babble the nonsense of one who is desperate for release:

'Do it to me, my lord; please do it to me; harder, no – softer, gentler; now harder again . . . Oh, fuck me, fuck me, I beg of you! Fill me up with your beloved manhood, split me with your thick shaft, make me scream with pleasure!'

I had meant to bring the girl off with my finger, but her entreaties were so heart-rending that I could hardly refuse her. So I threw her roughly across the wooden table, sending goblets and plates of food scattering across the surface, with such a clatter that I feared the servants would come running to see what was amiss. Then I laid her down with her back on the table, and her backside on the very edge, with her legs in the air. Aiming my now rock-hard prick carefully at the heart of her womanhood, I gave a mighty thrust; and was surprised to meet with resistance because of her tightness. It took me three good thrusts to get inside her, by which time she and I were both almost on the point of spending.

I rode her boldly, delighting in the submissiveness of such a high-born lady to my amorous assaults. And I quickly brought her to a climax which would have had her crying the castle down, had I not silenced her cries with a hand over her mouth.

Next, without even giving her time to recover, I pulled her off the table and turned her round, making her lie face down with her legs wide apart.

'What are you going to do now, my lord?' breathed Gisela, panting once again with desire for me.

'I am going to ride you in another way, my lady,' I replied, using some of the copious juices flowing down her thighs to lubricate the wrinkled brown arsehole which was now the object of my attentions and my growing lust. I looked around the table, and saw a thick, firm sausage which would serve my purpose well. With a single, deft movement, I seized it and rammed it into my lady's moist vagina, stifling her cries once again and turning them into moans of pleasure by rubbing her rosebud of delight into wakeful stiffness.

I then forced apart milady's nether cheeks, and worked my turgid manhood into her tight virgin hole. I doubt not that it caused her pain, for she writhed beneath my torments; but as I at last broke through into her forbidden passage, she gave a great sigh of contentment; and thrust herself eagerly at me as I toiled away at her with fingers, prick and that most curious of dildos.

When at last I showered her with spunk, she joined me in a climax of her own abundant love-juices.

I rode the Lady Gisela hard, all night long; and none dared to disturb us, though I am sure some must have suspected our deeds. At dawn, we both returned to our own rooms. The following night, when the potion had worn off, I saw her again but she gave no sign that she even recalled what had transpired the previous evening.

On the third evening, the Prince Aelfrith rode home, and on the fourth he and the Lady Gisela were married in great state. He confided to me that the potions I had brought him had proved efficacious in both cases, and that he was more than satisfied with his bride, who seemed innocent and yet strangely knowing in the ways of the bedchamber.

As for the Lady Gisela, I hear tell that she is well pleased with her elderly husband, for his potency defies his years. I have no doubt that the love philtre is also playing its part.

Her contentment reached its peak a few months ago, when – barely nine months from her wedding day – she gave birth to a son. A son with pale blond hair and grey eyes, just like his father.

King Uriens

'So!' cried Arthur, turning in rage upon his knight Sir Kay. 'I believed you a trustworthy knight, and you betrayed me! Is this how I am rewarded for feeding and clothing you and raising you from the rank of a poor squire?'

'I . . .' stammered Kay, still utterly confused by what he had heard himself speak. Though he had meant to speak only good of himself, he had told the truth – and it was not a virtuous truth.

The veiled sorceress was standing beside Merlin now, evidently amused by the spectacle of the old man trying desperately to masturbate his terrifyingly engorged penis, and failing because his arms were grown so weak.

She turned to Sir Kay once more.

'Your King's displeasure is your own repayment for such lamentable behaviour,' she told him in mocking tones. 'For he shall surely never again entrust you with such an important mission.'

And Arthur was indeed glaring at Sir Kay, who

blushed and stammered and knew not where to look or what to say.

'Enough,' decreed the veiled lady, throwing back the sides of her starry cape to ensure that all the knights present were given a fine view of her magnificent body. 'There are more stories still to hear. And I know how much you are all longing for my embrace, lusting after the tender savagery of my lips, my arms, my breasts, my arse, my sex.

'Good King Uriens – tell me why is it that you sit at this table. You were once a king in your own kingdom.'

Uriens, an aged man with white hair and a long, snowy beard, answered in a voice tremulous with age:

'I made King Arthur a gift of my kingdom,' he explained. 'For his knights rid my realm of many dragons and outlaws and evil usurpers. And in return, the King gave me a fine castle and lands, and a place at Camelot as his adviser. And that is why I now sit here as a Knight of the Round Table.'

'I see,' said the veiled woman. 'Well, I scarcely think a greybeard such as you would make a fitting lover. If you have tales to tell, surely they must be of a far-off age when you were young and strong and your manhood led you by the nose.'

'Indeed no, madam,' replied the old King, 'For I have a tale of a recent exploit, of sweet flesh but newly enjoyed.'

'Tell us your tale,' commanded the sorceress, placing her hand upon his shoulder and greatly enjoying the visions which flooded into her from the old man's mind. 'Tell us of the witch Morgana.'

It was in the year following the great plague, two summers ago, when my fate crossed with that of the witch Morgana.

King Arthur had but lately summoned me to his presence, and announced to me his gift of the Castle Maris, a fine fortress sea-bound on three sides and perched loftily on the cliffs overlooking the ocean. I knew little of my new lands, save that they had formerly belonged to the Baron Ulfius, an ally of Arthur who had been killed in battle a year previously. His daughter, the Lady Morgana, had taken over the stewardship of his lands, and had been castellan of Maris this twelve-month.

Arthur smiled as he told me of the lady's surpassing beauty, and of her loneliness in her sea-bound retreat.

'My good fellow,' he said. 'You shall have company aplenty with the Lady Morgana to busy herself with your care. I doubt not that she shall devote herself utterly to your comfort.'

For my part, I had little interest in the young woman's physical endowments; for, as you can see, I am an old man and no longer in my prime. I had almost forgotten the delights of the flesh, so long was it since I had kissed a woman's naked flesh, or thrust my hardness into her. But I confess I was glad of the lady's companionship, for I feared loneliness and was pleased to have a housekeeper to attend to my comforts.

Little did I imagine the ways in which the Lady Morgana would torment and delight me . . .

I reached Castle Maris on the evening of the third day, tired and longing for food and rest. The castle stood on a rocky promontory, dominating the lands around it: standing dark and eerie against the setting sun, its central tower as proud and insolent as a young man's phallus, defiantly erect in the face of an old man's envious disapproval.

We rode to the gatehouse and demanded entrance, in the name of King Arthur of Camelot. The drawbridge was duly lowered and we rode across, through the main castle gate and into the inner bailey, where the Lady Morgana awaited us.

She was indeed a handsome woman, and as I gazed upon her beauty I could not help wondering why such a fine lady was not yet wedded to some young warrior who would give her the comfort she needed.

'Good evening, my Lady Morgana,' I saluted her, planting a gallant kiss upon her outstretched hand. Looking up, I saw that she was blushing as though with pleasure, though I could not for my life imagine why.

'Good evening, Your Majesty,' replied the comely castellan, curtseying so deeply before me that I could not help seeing the generous swell of her creamy breasts within their low-cut bodice. It seemed to me almost as though that was what she had intended.

'Your Majesty,' she continued in her sweet, husky voice which had charmed me already, 'I am entirely happy to welcome you to Castle Maris. I have been so lonely here since my father died. We were so close, and you are so very like him, my lord.'

And, to my great surprise, she planted a daughterly kiss upon my wrinkled old cheek before summoning her servants to carry my baggage up to my apartments.

My bedroom was sumptuously appointed, the centrepiece being a huge bed decorated with rich carvings, which when I examined them more closely proved to be of the most interesting and inspiring subjects: rutting stags and hinds, a unicorn with a hugely erect phallus, cornucopiae spilling their bounty and naked nymphs holding exotic orchids.

Exhausted as I was from my journey, I lay down upon the soft, feather-filled mattress and let my mind wander. Why, so inspiring were those carvings that I began to think back over my life, and the conquests which I had made as a young and powerful king.

Many were the women I had courted and bedded, from scullery-wenches and milkmaids to high-born noblewomen and princesses. I recalled with pleasure my first encounter, when I was a mere boy of sixteen. My father and mother, on the point of arranging a prestigious marriage for me with the daughter of a neighbouring prince, were anxious to ensure that I would be adequate to my role as a bridegroom. Knowing that I was innocent of all matters fleshly, they decided to contrive a liaison for me with an older woman of my father's court – the Lady Brangwen, wife of my father's Chancellor.

I of course had no knowledge of what was afoot, so when my mother suggested that I should call upon the Lady Brangwen for lessons in music and dancing, I in my innocence believed that these were the only accomplishments I was expected to master.

To my great surprise (and not a little interest) I arrived in the Lady Brangwen's apartments to find that she had dismissed all her servants and was awaiting my arrival clad only in a light robe of Cathay silk, which displayed clearly the outline of her crested nipples, slender waist, rounded hips and even the little swelling marking the tuft of hairs at the base of her belly.

I must have blushed crimson to the roots of my hair, for the lady smiled and laid her cool, white hand on my arm:

'Be at ease, my young prince. Nothing ill shall befall you, I promise. Today you shall know nothing but delight.'

I gazed up into her face and felt as though I were drowning in the deep pools of her dark eyes. And I wanted to drown.

'Shall we begin the lesson now?' I stammered, still not comprehending that I had not been brought here to learn dance steps.

'Why, what an eager pupil you are!' smiled the Lady Brangwen. 'But be still: and be assured that I shall teach you everything I know, everything you will need to know to acquit yourself well as a prince and as a bridegroom.'

'Shall I now put on my dancing shoes?' I asked, in all innocence.

'You have no need of extra clothing,' she replied. 'On the contrary, you are far too heavily dressed. Let me assist you to remove some of these heavy vestments.'

And she began to unfasten my girdle. Dumbfounded, I simply stood my ground and allowed her to do what she would. In fact, I even began to feel that I wished she would hurry, that she would tear off my clothes faster so that I would be naked before her. I knew not why, but all of a sudden I wanted to be naked with this woman with the dancing breasts and smouldering eyes.

I knew, of course, of the tricks that my manhood could play. I had long since discovered the delights of coaxing the fellow to unyielding stiffness and rubbing him until he spat forth his gratitude in warm, sticky gobbets. I had often wondered what it would feel like to be able to put him into my mouth and lick him to his pleasure – but alas, I was no acrobat, and I was far too shy a lad to seek my solace from some other's lips.

Now I began once again to wonder how it would feel to place my manhood's tip between a pair of soft, sweet lips. Only this time, the lips were those of the Lady Brangwen.

At last, I stood naked before her, my prick dancing a little jig on my belly as I gazed upon her loveliness, cloaked though it was by the pale blue silk gown.

'You are a handsome young man,' said Brangwen approvingly, running her soft hands over my shoulders and chest. 'Finely made and pleasing to the eye and to the touch. Would you like to find out how I look and feel?'

'What . . . what do you mean?' I blurted, blushing an even deeper red, for I had already grasped her meaning.

'Watch, and learn,' replied the Lady Brangwen; and she began to undress before me – a deed swiftly done, for, as I soon discovered, she was wearing nothing but the blue silk gown. No shift, no undergarment of any kind.

Her flesh was pink and white and beautiful – a sight I had never before seen. I hardly dared look upon her, let alone touch. But she took my timorous hand and guided it to her breast, bidding me run my fingers over the ripening rosebuds of her nipples. She gave a little gasp – of surprise or pleasure, I knew not which – as my fingers touched her warm flesh and began to explore it.

My other hand the Lady Brangwen took and guided down the downy slope of her belly to the dark triangle of her pubic hair. I toyed for a little while with the glossy brown curls, before she urged me to set off once again on my journey, sliding the edge of my hand between her thighs and into her hidden pleasure palace.

She slid her feet slightly apart, to make the passage easier, and my trembling hand slipped inside as easily as if the way had been made expressly for it. My head was reeling with the suddenness, the excitement, the desires which I felt coursing through me, wild and uncontrollable and unexpected. I was terrified, and yet entranced, bewitched by the irresistible need which had overwhelmed me and destroyed my gentlemanly resolve. Now all I desired was Brangwen to teach me the cadences of her breathing, the music of her kisses, the love dance of her loins against mine.

'Be not afraid,' murmured Brangwen, feeling the trembling of my hand against her secret places. She picked up a jug of wine from the table, and poured a little into a drinking horn:

'Here: drink this down. It will make you feel more at ease.'

Though I seldom drank wine, I seized the cup and, putting it to my lips, drained it dry. Brangwen refilled it and I drained it a second time. My head was beginning to swim, but I felt better already – braver and ready now for the fray.

Brangwen lay down on the edge of her bed, with her legs apart, and urged me to my knees before her, placing both of my hands upon her curly brown triangle.

'Do what you will,' she breathed. 'Explore my depths, and I shall guide you on your journey.'

I gazed upon her loveliness dumbfounded. Never before had I dreamed of such a sight, of such a playground for my youthful fingers. I began by stroking Brangwen's brown curls, bringing my face closer to them the better to appreciate their heady scent: a mingled perfume of sex and rosewater, which made me far drunker than the wine could ever have done.

'Kiss me; kiss me there,' urged Brangwen, half sitting so that she could hold my head and direct it towards her mossy triangle. 'Breathe in the fragrance; let it waft you into the music of my being, the music of love.'

I buried my face in her curls, breathing deeply so that her scent entered me like incense or the richest tapestry of music in a fine cathedral, that bids hearts and minds rise towards Heaven. And rise I did; for my own instrument was primed and well-tuned, ready to play its own sweet tune, to harmonise with Brangwen's counterpoint. My own dear flute stood stiff and proud against my belly, and begged only for hand or lips or cunny-hole to bring forth its tribute of music.

I put out my tongue a little, and burrowed it into the hair. My efforts were rewarded with an appreciative sigh, so I became bolder and resolved to see what other notes I could bring forth.

Exploring with my fingers, I found that my Lady Brangwen's secret parts opened like a flower, with two big scented petals, which when parted revealed a moist heart dripping with honeydew. Eagerly I lapped up some of this liquid, and found it heavenly-sweet and utterly refreshing. As my tongue explored, it happened upon a little hard nubbin of flesh, like the stamen of the flower; and as my tongue passed over it, my Lady Brangwen gave a great groan so that I believed I must have hurt her, and withdrew in confusion.

'Oh no, no!' she cried. 'Do not stop, I beg of you! For you have found the very heart of my music. Only toy with it some more, and you shall see what pretty tunes it plays!'

Reassured, I returned to my contemplation of the delights before me, licking the little nubbin delicately and all the while exploring with my fingers. I found a hole, which seemed tiny from the outside; but as I toyed with it I found it grew wider at my touch, and – to my immense surprise and delight – swallowed up three of my fingers without the slightest difficulty. Oh, how my Lady Brangwen sang at my touch! I felt as though I were the most skilful of minstrels, striking heavenly chords from a golden lyre.

How astonished I was when, with a loud cry, my Lady Brangwen fell back on to the bed. I felt the velvet-soft rings of her hole opening and closing on my fingers, and more fragrant liquor came washing over my hand and tongue.

I pulled away from Brangwen, and climbed on to the bed beside her, a little afraid that I had harmed her in some way or done something that I should not have done.

'What ails thee, my Lady Brangwen?' I asked of her, anxiously.

But she opened her eyes and smiled sweetly at me. With a little laugh, she said: 'Sweet Uriens, know you not what you have done?'

I shook my head, rather glumly.

'You have given me the sweetest gift that ever man gave woman: the gift of ecstasy. You have played the most heavenly music upon me, and there is yet more to play.'

Seeing that I clearly did not quite understand, she

went on: 'You have toyed with your own body to give it pleasure?'

I blushed.

'Yes, of course you have. You have rubbed your little flute here until the sweetest notes gushed forth from it.' And she took hold of my rock-hard penis and began to rub it. 'Well, know you now that women too can play sweet music upon their bodies. That little bud of flesh you licked and the slippery tunnel where you buried your fingers, are the keys to that music, the strings of the harp.'

All of a sudden, I felt my crisis upon me, and was quite unable to stop myself spurting out my pleasure all over Brangwen's belly.

'Oh, I am so sorry!' I cried, blushing crimson with shame as I gasped out the last of my seed.

'Why be ashamed of what is natural and good?' Brangwen laid me down upon the bed and knelt astride my belly, with her face towards my feet. Before I realised what was happening she had taken my still-hard penis into her mouth and was coaxing it back into full rigidity. Never in my young life had I seen any minstrel play such a perfect flourish on an instrument as the Lady Brangwen played that day upon my fleshy flute. And lo! it was my turn to sing.

She seemed able to sense that my joy was approaching, and – to my great disappointment – withdrew her delightful lips from my manhood just as the seed was about to rise up my shaft. Was she, I wondered, going to deprive me of this second crisis of pleasure, which I sensed would be even more intense than the first?

But I need not have feared; for she had other, still more exciting, adventures in store for me. Putting her arms tenderly around me, she kissed me passionately and then urged me to climb on top of her. Reaching down my belly, she took hold of my prick and guided it towards her hole. Willingly, if clumsily, I followed her lead and thrust into her, gasping with delight as I felt myself sliding into the moist warmth of her belly.

'Fuck me, oh, fuck me!' cried Brangwen, clutching at my arse-cheeks and governing the speed of my ride: slow and leisurely, so that I did not come too quickly and spoil her own joy.

My head was still spinning as I thrust in and out of Brangwen, my first woman, my very first fuck. We sang together in celestial harmonies as we rose towards our shared and glorious pleasure; and afterwards, I lay panting upon her belly, with my head pillowed on those beautiful soft breasts, until Brangwen awoke my desires once again, and we retuned to our instruments anew.

I was awakened from my dream by the sound of a knock at my bedroom door. Still dazed from sleep, I called out:

'Enter.'

The door swung open, to reveal the Lady Morgana, clad in a clinging blood-red velvet gown which accentuated the milky-white swell of her generous bosom. She carried a candle, for it had grown dark now; and its light cast strange shadows on my bed-head, making the nymphs seem to run faster from their satyric pursuers, and the unicorns' gilded horns gleam almost menacingly in the twilight.

'Good evening, Your Majesty,' breathed the lovely Morgana, who seemed to glide into the room, so smoothly and sinuously did she move. She was loose-limbed and tall, with an easy grace which reminded me of my own Queen when I had wedded her, all those years ago.

To my surprise, I found that I was no longer tired. Indeed, in recent years my rest had never been so refreshing. I felt invigorated, revitalised, almost youthful. Why! One might almost believe that such a bed had magical powers, that the carved images of rampant sexuality actually had the power to communicate themselves to the sleeper, to arouse within him desires which he had not known for years past: desires, and the ability to fulfil them.

Yes, for the first time in years I realised that my hitherto flaccid manhood was beginning to rise to attention beneath my robes, eager to pay its homage to the Lady Morgana's beauty. But I was an old man, and she was beautiful and but recently bereaved. It would be unthinkable, and most unseemly. And besides, surely I had lost all interest in pleasures carnal many years since.

The Lady Morgana placed the candle upon a wooden clothes-chest and then sat down on the edge of the bed where I lay, trembling with apprehension.

'So very like my dear departed father,' she murmured taking my hand and placing it against her lips. 'We were so close, you know. But alas! So many of my games that he would not play; for he thought them unseemly between father and daughter. But you, my dear King Uriens, are not my father.'

I was more than a little alarmed at such talk. In what devilish practices had this young women attempted to persuade her father to join her? And what alchemy had she practised upon me, that my tired, old member should so willingly rise to greet her; that my body should yearn to be uncovered by her and kissed to ecstasy?

'My father was a learned man,' continued Morgana, still caressing my hand. Her moonstone ring gleamed with an inner fire that seemed to draw me on, ever faster, to my own perdition. 'He taught me all he knew of worlds seen and unseen, of science and alchemy and the esoteric arts. I spent all my days with him, learning at his knee. And that is why I have never married, Your Majesty; for never did I find a man to compare with my dear father. But you . . . You are so very like him.'

'I . . . I am very tired,' I stammered, wondering how I could extricate myself from this embarrassment with as much dignity as possible. 'The journey has quite exhausted me,' I lied, hoping that she would understand me and leave. 'I should like to rest.'

'Oh, my dear King!' exclaimed Morgana. 'Are you not refreshed after your slumbers on my father's bed?' It is generally most efficacious in restoring the mind and body to its full power. The mattress is filled with a secret blend of magical herbs, and the bed itself is carved from aromatic woods, each of which has special powers to charm and restore. You must indeed be exhausted if it has not at all revived you.'

She was looking at me rather slyly, I felt; and I knew that I had not concealed my interest in her – for my still-swelling manhood was clearly visible through the folds of my robes. Something told me that this young woman had powers beyond my mortal ken, and which I should never succeed in resisting. Whatever Morgana wanted of me, she would have it that night, whether I would give it willingly or no.

Now Morgana was beginning to explore my body: at first gently and cautiously, but then more boldly and lewdly with each passing second.

'See!' she cried delightedly, stroking my ankle. 'This ankle is just like my father's ... and these calves. You have such beautiful legs – well formed and yet slender, almost delicate.' Gently, she lifted the hem of my robe so that it was up round my waist. Despite my great confusion, I seemed to have lost the will to resist this woman's seductive powers, and I simply lay quite still and allowed her to have her will of me as she lifted my robe higher and drew it off over my head.

Besides which, I was beginning, in spite of myself, to enjoy the experience ...

'Oh, how handsome you are!' cried Morgana, much to my secret amusement, for as you know I am an old man now, and my body is not in the flower of its youth. 'Such a beautiful body: may I kiss it?'

And, without waiting for my answer, Morgana bent over me and began to apply the tenderest of kisses to my limbs, throat and breast.

'Father so loved me to soothe his skin with kisses,' explained Morgana. 'It is so hot and burdensome, toiling in an alchemist's workshop. After a long day's work, he would often lay him down on this very bed, and ask me to run my lips and tongue over his body, to cool his flesh.'

And delicious it was, too. But the touch of her tongue upon my body did not soothe or quieten its heat: on the contrary, it awakened yet more, unbidden desires within me, and I grew hot with lust, my poor neglected prick rearing its head in vain. For, though she circled my loins many times with her delicate kisses, not once did she touch my most intimate parts.

As though reading my mind, Morgana raised her eyes to mine and spoke:

'Alas, there was one thing which my father would

not allow me to do for him, though I swear it would have soothed him far better than any other service I could have done him. But *you* will allow me to do it to you, will you not? For I would not wish my father's fate upon you, Your Majesty . . .'

I gave a shudder of fear. What could she possibly mean? Did she wish me ill? Surely her father had died in battle? Or had that story been told abroad to conceal some other, far more sinister truth?

I had no opportunity for further thought, for the Lady Morgana was upon me like a wolverine, taking my manhood into her mouth and tormenting it with her lips and tongue whilst she massaged my stones with her red-tipped talons.

For the first time in more years than I dared remember, I felt the seed swelling my stones, and their velvety pouch growing tighter as they prepared to give forth their bounty. As my seed fountained forth into Morgana's mouth, it felt as though some bright star had exploded inside my head, and – in an agony of exquisite pleasure – I fell back on the bed in a deep swoon.

When I opened my eyes, Morgana had gone; and only my own nakedness remained to remind me of what had passed between us. The night was chill, and I slipped under the bedclothes, pulling them tight up under my chin. The candle had burned out, leaving the room in darkness save for the pale light of the moon, which filtered in through the casement window, casting an eerie sheen over all.

I knew not if I woke or swooned, for I felt as though I were floating in an unreal world of formless phantoms, of moving shadows that were neither good nor evil, neither alive nor dead.

As I gazed towards the stars, I saw the casement

window swing open and a dark shape cross the moon. As it drew nearer, I saw that it was a large bat, which flew in through the window and circled my bed, as though it had a message for me.

As I watched in horrified apprehension, it seemed to me that the bat disappeared, leaving behind a small white cloud which expanded until it was the height of a man. Little by little, the mist cleared, resolving itself into the form of an old man, white-bearded and naked save for a wreath of yew-branches about his brow, his phallus menacingly erect. He carried a heavy grimoire of learned spells.

The old man raised his right hand and pointed his finger at me. Then his toothless mouth opened and he spoke to me:

'Beware, King Uriens. Beware the fate the witch Morgana has in store for thee. For her carnal lusts are insatiable, her demands never-ceasing. She will bleed thee dry, old man, as she did her own father.'

And suddenly the image was gone, and I was alone once again in the empty room, pondering on the strange significance of the old man's words.

The following day, I avoided the Lady Morgana as far as I could, and busied myself with organising my men and possessions as they were installed in my new home. But she came to me in the evening, and bade me very tenderly come with her to her workshop, wherein she carried on her late father's work. I dared not ask her what had truly happened to her father, for I feared the nature of that truth.

Morgana's workshop was in one of the dungeons that lay beneath Castle Maris, connected to the sea by a warren of tunnels which had long provided an escape route for brigands and besieged castle defenders.

I found Morgana toiling beside a brazier on which a crucible of molten metal was bubbling. As I approached, she lifted it from the hot coals with a blacksmith's tongs and poured the metal into a small mould. As it cooled, I saw that it was glowing yellow.

'Gold!' I cried, astonished.

Morgana smiled.

'It is indeed, Your Majesty. For my father discovered the famed Philosopher's Stone. And now the secret shall be yours, for you are the new lord of Castle Maris. The secret shall be yours alone, if only you will take my father's place beside me.'

Her eyes were burning into mine, and I felt myself grow weak; and try as I might, I could not keep my eyes open. The last thing I remember is lying on the cold stone floor of the workshop, and Morgana forcing a few drops of a bitter liquid between my unwilling lips.

When I awoke, I could not at first distinguish where I was. A loud roaring sound filled my head, and I shook it – but the sound remained. I opened my eyes. It was dark all around me, but the moon illuminated the scene. I was lying naked on the beach at the base of the cliffs, with Castle Maris looming up above me.

Standing over me was the Lady Morgana, naked also, her long black hair unplaited and falling over shoulders and back, so that her beautiful white breasts seemed to surge forth out of a fleecy black cloud: a cloud as black as her own soul.

She was chanting strange words in a language I could not comprehend: but as she spoke them, desires rose in my loins and my manhood sprang to attention, like a lapdog ready to adore its mistress. I tried to move but I could not, for my arms and legs felt like lead. All I could think of was how it would feel

93

to be inside the Lady Morgana, and how it had felt to explode inside her mouth the night before.

'My dear King Uriens,' murmured Morgana, gazing down upon me with her coal-black, glittering eyes. 'I have you at last. But this poor member will not serve. Let us see what better we can do.' And, bending to touch the tip of my penis with a willow wand, she spoke another strange incantation which made the blood boil in my veins, the seed in my loins.

And all at once, my manhood began to grow. At first, it swelled only until it touched my navel; but then it continued to grow and swell, thickening and lengthening until it was the breadth of a man's wrist and a full cubit long. I cried out in mingled horror and pleasure: for whilst the sight repelled me, the divine sensations had magnified in proportion to the size of my prick, and truly I was in a heavenly Hell of expectation.

Without further ado, the witch Morgana bestrode me with her fine sturdy limbs. I felt I must surely split her with my massive prick, but to my amazement and delight she stretched without difficulty to accommodate it, and she swallowed me up to the hilt. I thought that I must surely be causing her pain, but she laughed wildly as she began to ride my prick with merry gusto.

Old as I was, I could not but respond to her expert's touch, and I soon spurted into her belly a tribute of foaming abundance.

'More, more!' she cried.

'But I am spent!' I pleaded. 'And I am an old man – I can no more!'

But Morgana was implacable. She bent over me and administered three more drops of the bitter liquid, whereupon my prick grew more massive still and I felt as though my stones would burst for the abundance of seed within them.

She climbed on to me again, and again I felt my massive prick sliding up inside her belly.

Three more times Morgana brought me to orgasm, and we cried out together in our ecstasy. But I am an old man, and with each successive climax I felt my life's blood thin, my heart grow weaker. And I knew, in my soul, that she would ride me until she killed me, until my heart burst and I gasped out my last breath upon the cold, wet sand.

At that moment, I looked up into the sky and saw a bat circling our heads. It hung there for a moment, then swooped down upon us, as though to do us harm. Morgana shrieked angrily and leapt to her feet, trying to beat it off with her hands. I, for my part, took my chance and looked for ways of flight. Turning, to my amazement I saw a silver sword appear upon the sand, and I picked it up. It was light, but razor sharp and deadly. I looked at Morgana and saw that the bat was at her throat, as though trying to bite into her flesh and drain her of her life blood. I knew that I should take my chance and flee, or better still, leave the bat to slay the witch Morgana. But I remembered the delights I had known with her, and I swung the sword instead at the bat, which fell dying upon the sand.

To my horror, as the bat's body hit the sand it was transformed into the body of an old man, white-bearded and naked save for a wreath of yew branches. For a brief moment, the old man's eyes fluttered open and he murmured to me in gratitude:

'Blessings upon you, for you have released me at last.'

Then he fell back, dead, upon the sand.

'Father!' shrieked Morgana, falling upon the corpse and covering it in kisses. 'What have I done? I meant only to imprison you for a while, until you came to see the rightness of my desires.'

And I turned upon my heel and fled, back into the tunnels beneath the cliffs, and away from Castle Maris; vowing that I should never more return.

Sir Erek

A rthur and his knights sat in stunned amazement. 'And so, once again the cunning wiles of women overcome our better natures,' observed Arthur, drily.

'Looking back, I regret not one moment of it all,' replied Uriens, defiantly. 'If she abused me, well, it was a fair exchange for the pleasure I knew in her arms.'

'Bravely said, King Uriens,' applauded the veiled sorceress. 'Perhaps you are not such an unworthy suitor, after all. Though your frail form would not long endure. Perhaps your punishment, old man, is that your body can never fully accomplish what your heart desires.

'And let us turn now to brave Sir Erek, who is so tall and strong and fearless. What have you to tell us, Sir Knight?'

'I have nothing to hide from you, thou fiend in woman's form,' he replied fiercely, desperately trying to reach for his sword and failing though he strove with all his might.

'Is that so? Then I bid you, Sir Erek, tell us all the tale of your wife Enid. The tale of a faithful wife, scorned and sorely tried.'

Erek opened his mouth to protest, and to proclaim the slander upon his name; but as his lips parted to speak, the truth forced itself up from the depths of his heart, and would not be denied.

THE TALE OF SIR EREK AND HIS WIFE ENID

I married my wife Enid two years ago, and was with her but one short week before my lord the King bade me journey overseas to Palestine, there to fight for the holy cause. I did not return until almost a year later, and as I rode towards my manor, my heart was full of fear lest all was not well. I feared especially that my young wife might have betrayed me with another during my absence, and though I had no cause to doubt her, my heart burst with jealousy.

Enid came running to greet me, and was most loving and attentive. But I could not rid my mind of the terrible fear that she had deceived me. All about her I saw pretty boys and handsome men, and I convinced myself that she had been bedded by one of them, if not by all.

And so I determined to find a means of testing the limits of my wife's fidelity.

The following morning, I awoke beside my wife and looked upon her once more with the eyes of jealousy. Had another man's head graced my pillow? Had another man's prick slipped joyfully into Enid's moist womanhood and taken its delight there?

My wife's eyes fluttered open, and she smiled at me.

'Good morrow, husband,' she said; then she noticed my troubled aspect. 'What ails three, my sweet Lord Erek?'

'Thou art a false jade, to lie there and beguile me with thy smiles and soft words and caresses,' I replied, the jealousy in my heart turning to anger and thirst for vengeance. 'For well I know the true nature of thy "innocence". Thou has offered thy delight to all men whilst I have been fighting for the Holy City.'

'No, no!' she cried, pale horror draining the colour from her face. 'Thou art mistaken, my lord. I am ever true to thee!'

But I would not listen, and I turned to her and spoke coldly:

'If thou art indeed a true wife, thou shalt prove your loyalty by obeying me in all things.'

'In all things, my lord. Only ask, and it shall be done.'

'Then arise and dress, and follow me. There are tasks for you to perform.'

I bade her dress herself in her most alluring finery. Then I took her roughly by the arm and dragged her through the house to the kitchen, where the greasy cook Hilde was stirring the pot of gruel upon the fire, whilst her scabby potboy turned the spit on which was roasting a side of freshly killed venison.

Hilde and the boy gazed at us in astonishment, for it was but seldom that the lord and lady of the house demeaned themselves by visiting the kitchens.

I called Hilde over and bid her strip before me, a request she carried out readily, if a little quizzically; for although she attended often to the carnal needs of the village lads and my men-at-arms, never before had I asked for a share in her favours.

She was, I must confess it, a buxom and comely

woman in her middle years – rosy-cheeked and full-bosomed, with a fine broad backside which my leather-gloved hand fair itched to know more intimately. So vivid were the images it brought to mind, that I could almost feel the hot moistness of her intimate furrow, the resolute tightness of a forbidden hole which so many had breached.

But it was not Hilde that I had come to see. My sport would be of a more refined and piquant nature. I turned to my wife Enid, who seemed utterly perplexed by my actions – as did the unlovely potboy, who was feigning great interest in his work at the spit, but was squinting sidelong at the naked cook and no doubt wondering what might happen next.

'Come, Enid,' I commanded her. 'Take off your finery and put on these more fitting clothes which Hilde has taken off. Hilde shall deck herself in your cast-off finery; and for today, you shall be cook and she shall be the lady of this house.'

As Enid seemed rather loth to comply, I hastened her obedience by taking off her golden girdle and forcing open the laces which held her gown tight across her slender back.

With tears in her eyes, Enid began slowly to undress before me. It was indeed a strange and exciting sight to see my elegant and fragile wife stripped of her finery and standing naked and trembling in the middle of the filthy, rush-strewn kitchen floor.

Hilde bent down and picked up Enid's finery, eagerly trying it for size. Of course, the clothes were too small for her and the fine brocade gown was stretched like a child's across her ample frame, her sweating, grubby flesh bulging betwen the laces in a grotesque parody of a fine lady.

Weeping copiously now, Enid began to pull on the cook's malodorous garb – a shift grown grey with sweat and dirt, full of holes and crawling with lice; greasy leather slippers and a tattered dun-coloured woollen gown with a dirty linen apron.

Well satisfied with what I saw, I sat me down on a rough wooden bench and addressed Hilde:

'My Lady Hilde, you are the queen of this culinary palace for the day. This poor slut Enid is your slave, your new scullery maid. As you can see, she is a slatternly girl, yet has airs and graces which needs must be beaten out of her. Only hard work will cleanse her of her sluttish behaviour and teach her the true path of redemption. She knows nothing, poor girl. You must teach her as you choose. She is yours to direct. I shall not interfere – only observe.'

Hilde curtsied to me and cast me a knowing smile. For – little did my wife Enid know – I had already spoken to the cook of my plan, and all her bewilderment was a skilful feint for Enid's benefit. In fact, we had worked out the details of my revenge most thoroughly in advance, and I knew that all would proceed to our complete satisfaction, Hilde comprehending perfectly my taste for interesting sexual pursuits and mortification of the flesh.

'But, my lord!' cried Enid, her arms stretched out to me in supplication. 'What have I done to offend thee?'

'Silence, wench!' cried Hilde, dealing her a sound slap across the face. 'Know your station and do not speak to your betters unless you are spoken to. Now – on your knees and scrub the hearth. I shall be watching you and if you do anything wrong . . . Beware!'

Still sobbing, poor Enid fell to her knees and began

101

scrubbing away at the filthy hearth, which of course the cunning Hilde had made especially foul with dirt and grease. The poor lass broke her nails and roughened her fragile white skin as she put her soul into her work. But at every turn she served only to incite the cook to louder insults and greater violence.

'Slut!' cried the cook, taking a leather strap from the wall and swinging back her arm the better to take aim. 'Can you do nothing?'

And she brought down the strap upon poor Enid's back and buttocks. Even through the woollen gown the pain must have been intense, and my pulse quickened at the thought of the discomfort which my accomplice was inflicting on this temptress who had first bewitched and then cuckolded me. My prick began to stiffen and I caressed it surreptitiously beneath the riding-cloak I had laid across my knees. I did not wish to show too early how this unusual sport pleased and excited me.

'I . . . I can do no more!' cried poor Enid, falling forward on to the still-dirty stones of the hearth her shoulders heaving with sobs.

'Lazy slattern!' thundered Hilde. 'What use are you to me as a kitchen wench if you refuse to work and have no mind to learn?'

'I am sorry,' sobbed Enid. But her mistress was grown implacable, and would show her no mercy.

'Let us see if a keener taste of the strap will quicken your hands,' she said, and turned to the potboy, whose eyes were as round as full moons in his silly head. 'Lift up her skirts,' she commanded him.

With trembling fingers, the potboy obeyed. It was plain to see he had never before touched a woman, let alone a fine lady like Enid. It pleased me enormously to see the bulge of his adolescent penis, swelling and begging for escape from his woollen hose.

The boy took hold of Enid's skirts and hoisted them up over her head, revealing the two perfect half-moons of her dimpled backside, already lightly steaked with red after the savage beating that Hilde had given her.

Turning up the incongruous lace and brocade sleeves of her gown, Hilde set to work with a will upon her unwilling pupil, determined to knock all the silly fancies out of her head. The first blow of the strap made Enid arch her back and cry out in pain, but the strip of wood which the potboy thrust between her teeth muffled her subsequent cries.

I began to rub my prick harder and harder as I watched the scene laid out before me for my enter-tainment: my wife, in the garb of a sluttish kitchen wench, was lying face down amid the muck and rubbish of the kitchen floor, her martyred backside thrusting into the air to receive the punishment inflicted upon it by my accomplice, while the potboy held down her arms to prevent any attempt at escape.

To my surprise and interest, I noticed Enid's resist-ance easing off as the blows became harder and her buttocks redder. I wondered if she had merely re-signed herself to the pain. But I could not help noticing that, with each successive blow, her legs were sliding fractionally further apart – so that, eventually, I could clearly glimpse the tempting wet furrow between her milky thighs.

It seemed that Hilde too had noticed this apparent offering, for she decided to make good use of it. Bending down, she put away the strap and instead picked up a long-handled wooden spoon which she used to stir the cauldron when it sat upon the fire. It was a rough-carved implement, with a handle as thick as a man's penis.

Without warning, Hilde took the handle of the spoon and inserted it between Enid's thighs, taking no heed of the poor girl's faint cries of distress as the dry wood martyred her tender places.

'Slut!' she cried. 'Since you would have yourself stuffed full to the brim, take this into your cunny-hole!' And she guided the handle of the spoon to the gate of Enid's womanhood, and thrust it home into Enid's sex.

Evidently Enid had not been entirely indifferent to her chastisement, for her cunt was moist and did not resist the entry of the wooden handle into its tender depths. On the contrary, she began to thrust back-wards a little, as though to swallow up ever more of the hard, dry wood and so take her pleasure from it. More than ever, I was convinced that I had not judged my wife unfairly – for here she was, beaten and humiliated on the filthy kitchen floor, and yet begging the fat greasy cook to masturbate her harder and harder with the wooden handle of a serving-ladle.

'Take that, slut!' cried Hilde, ramming the handle as far home as it would go.

And with her other hand, she began to torment my lady Enid's virgin arsehole, using her nails to tease the flesh and spitting upon the dry hole to make it easier to insert her finger inside it.

And so it was that, with a wooden spoon-handle in her vagina and the tip of a finger wriggling its way into her arse, my lady Enid came to orgasm on the filthy kitchen floor, her love juice inundating the wooden handle.

'On your feet, slut! There is work to do,' commanded Hilde, pulling the still-dazed Enid to her feet and pulled her dress down over her hips. She stood and swayed, forced to hold on to the edge of a table to prevent herself from falling over, seemingly quite unaware that one of her bubbies had escaped from the low-cut bodice of her dress and was poking its pink-nosed muzzle into the greedy face of the potboy, who was quite clearly desperate to take it into his mouth.

'What is it that you want of me now?' pleaded Enid, her voice scarcely more than a hoarse whisper. 'What must I do to turn away your wrath?'

'Why, that is a more sensible attitude, my girl!' replied the cruel-minded cook. 'Well, let me see. I think that your first task should be to help young Oric here to turn the spit.'

The potboy gazed first at Hilde and then at Enid, in a mixture of disbelief, terror and gratitude.

'Show her what to do, Oric,' commanded Hilde. 'She is yours to instruct, as you please. You may do with her whatever you think fit. Whatever pleases you.'

Oric was not slow to understand and profit from his good fortune.

'Bend over,' he said, 'and turn the spit.' And he placed the lady Enid's right hand upon the handle, showing her how to turn it. Her left he placed on the growing bulge of his prick, making her caress him through the woollen fabric of his hose.

As she turned the heavy spit, she was forced to bend forward, and – with a little help from eager young Oric – both of her bubbies had soon bounced free of their restraint, and were bobbing merrily before his face. Oric took the right nipple into his mouth, and tweaked the left between finger and thumb, causing the poor lass to cry out in a mixture of pain and pleasure.

'Well done, my lad. Instruct her as you will. But mark well, she is a slow learner. You have to force your will upon her.'

So young was Oric, and so hot blooded and seldom relieved of his burden, that he knew he could not long withstand the twin delights of having Enid's hand on his prick and her nipple in his mouth. With each caress, each suck, he felt his manhood growing stiffer and more engorged, and knew that his crisis was not far away. But everything in him cried out for a more intimate consummation of his great good fortune.

Reluctantly, Oric pulled away from Enid and moved her hand temporarily from his cock. Swiftly, he pulled down the front of his hose and revealed a surprisingly impressive shaft, flanked by two beautiful, downy bollocks in a large, velvety purse of flesh. For the first time in my life, I actually found myself envying the kitchen potboy, and longing to enjoy what he was about to enjoy. As I rubbed my ever-hardening shaft (carefully, so as not to bring myself too soon to my crisis) I even found myself wondering what it would be like to have them both: fragile, sobbing Enid and the greasy, lustful potboy together, playing with my prick and toying with my balls. For I had never had a man or a boy, and the prospect intrigued me.

But Oric had no thought for me. His eyes were all for the lovely Jezebel, the high-born slut Enid, who was still bent over the spit, her pink tipped titties hanging and quivering as she turned the handle and gasped with the exertion of it. Before she knew what was happening to her, Oric had lifted up her skirts and was running his greedy young hands all over her marbled backside, feeling the heat which I knew must be emanating from that martyred flesh, running his fingers ever closer to the furrow until at last they slipped between her buttocks.

Enid gasped as she felt Oric's fingers exploring her from stem to stern.

'No!' she cried. 'Please . . . No . . .'

But Hilde snapped out a command: 'Be still, harlot! And be attentive to your instruction. Oric is your master now. You must obey him, or taste the strap again.' And she flexed the tough, thick leather strap between her hands, showing Enid its suppleness, its pain-dealing power.

Enid was silent now, her eyes demurely lowered; utterly submitted to the chastisement about to be vented upon her.

Oric needed no further encouragement. He pulled Enid's hand from the spit and drew it backwards until it rested upon the hard smoothness of his erect penis, urging her to masturbate him by guiding her hand with his own. She made no attempt to draw away, and allowed herself to milk the young boy's shaft until at last he drew away, afraid no doubt that he would come to orgasm before he had enjoyed this magnificent and unexpected prize with which he had been so suddenly endowed.

Taking hold of Enid's arse-cheeks, Oric felt roughly for the soft wetness of her hole; then he placed the tip of his prick against it and thrust firmly into her. Poor little Enid cried out with the harshness of her treatment, but wriggle and writhe as she might, she could no more free herself than could some poor little mouse in the jaws of a marauding cat.

Oric took his pleasure roughly and greedily, caring

not a jot for his poor victim, who moaned piteously as he clutched at her soft, pink-tipped bubbies and drove pitilessly into the very heart of her. He heeded not her cries, nor let her escape one second from his grasp. As he drove into her, I distinctly heard the slap of his stones against my Lady Enid's backside, and the light squelching as his prick rammed in and out of his victim's well-anointed cunny-hole.

For I now saw clearly that my lady did not find her ravishment distasteful. Her juices had begun to flow, and she was thrusting her arse backwards to meet her violator's invading cock. The jade – I knew for certain now that she had indeed deceived me; but I no longer cared, for the pleasure I was deriving from this lewd and unusual sport was far greater than I had ever enjoyed in my lady wife's embrace. It excited me beyond measure to know that my wife was being violated by a filthy potboy; that she could feel his rough hands clutching at her soft white breasts, his hot, rancid breath on the back of her delicate swan's neck, his fat, greedy cock in her tight wet womanhood.

I heard young Oric's breath quicken, and he cried out in his youthful ecstasy:

'I die, I die . . . Oh, mercy upon me, for I die!'

And with a final, massive thrust, he clutched Enid to him as his copious seed pumped into her belly. So aroused was I by such a glorious sight that I came myself, flooding the palm of my hand with such a torrent as made my poor head spin.

I at once felt a great surge of regret; for I had not wanted to end my adventure so soon. But I need not have worried; for the very sight of Enid's martyred buttocks, as Oric withdrew from her, set my manhood leaping once more for the heavens. Oh! How I shivered with delight to see her thighs, soiled with this vulgar youth's seed. I watched it running in rivulets down the white flesh, and imagined what it would be like to lick the seed from her flesh, to taste her where another man had taken his pleasure; and afterwards, to take my own pleasure there, driving into her until she begged for mercy. And even then refusing to heed her cries.

It was Hilde who broke the silence.

'You shall yet learn, hussy,' she said in tones of haughty condescension. 'But it will take much time, much pain of your part. Now: back to your duties, slut. There is work for you to do. The men will soon be in from the fields for refreshment.'

Enid was set to work gathering up the soiled rushes and replacing them with fresh ones. Her tear-stained face was no longer deathly pale, but flushed and hot, and her eyes held a strange brightness.

At that moment, the door to the kitchen swung open, and in strode two of the villeins who worked on my demesne: Aluf, a straw-haired Saxon, and Gunnar, a tall, broad-shouldered Northman with an evil-looking scar slashed across his face where his left eye ought to be. I knew that they had come for a very special type of refreshment; for the cook Hilde offered her favours to them whenever they wished it. Today, it would not be Hilde who attended to their needs.

'Up, slut, and bring a pitcher of ale,' commanded Hilde, smiling side-long at the men who were eyeing her in her new finery with no little surprise. 'As you see, we have a new kitchen wench today,' she told them. 'A little slatternly, but a swift learner. She will serve you today, good sirs. Whatever your need or want, you have only to ask, to take.'

'Ale, slut!' demanded Gunnar, lowering himself on to the low wooden bench which flanked the table. Enid hurried to him with a massive earthenware pitcher of ale, stumbling a little in her anxiety so that a few drops spilled on to Gunnar's leather leggings.

Immediately the giant Northman seized Enid by the arm and pulled her to her knees.

'Clumsy slut! Lick it up.' And he forced her head down between his legs, so that her face touched the leather where it covered his powerful thighs. Obediently, she put out her tongue and lapped up the spilt ale.

'Higher, slut!' He forced her head higher up, towards his groin, making sure that she knew what he desired and demanded of her. With his free hand, he fumbled beneath the hem of his jerkin and succeeded in unfastening the laces which held his leather leggings in place.

As the leather parted, his thick, purple-headed penis sprang into view; and he used his fingers to prise apart Enid's reluctant lips, guiding his stiffness into her mouth. Now that he had both hands free, he used them to prevent the poor girl from escaping him; moving her head backwards and forwards to govern the rhythm of her ministrations, and all the time instructing and chastising her:

'Faster, slut. No . . . Slower now. Careful with those sharp little teeth, or you shall feel my belt upon your back. Now – run your tongue over the tip . . . Yes, yes . . . And suck harder, harder . . .'

Whilst this was happening, Aluf had poured himself a cup of ale and drained it with obvious relish as he beheld the delightful sight before him. Once refreshed, he threw himself into the fray with a will, unfastening his own leggings and taking out a finely formed prick whose glistening tip spoke volumes about his enjoyment of the situation.

Kneeling down behind Enid, Aluf hoisted up her skirts once more and gazed appreciatively upon her still-marbled backside.

'I see you know well the way to discipline your kitchen wenches,' he murmured, running rough fingers over the still-tender flesh. 'Now let us see if we cannot teach her another valuable lesson.'

And he pulled apart the Lady Enid's nether cheeks, and felt for her cunny-hole, thrusting into her with the casual need that simply takes what it desires, without thought.

Enid was learning her part. She did not flinch under her torturer's rod, allowing him to ride her like a favourite mare, without complaint or resistance. He took her quickly, and then withdrew to stroke his shaft back to stiffness as he watched his companion pour forth his tribute into the poor slut's mouth, smiling as she coughed and spluttered and sought to swallow his abundance.

'We have yet time,' announced Gunnar, glancing through the window. 'The sun is not yet high in the skies. The wench may yet serve us another time.'

And he and his companion took hold of Enid and stripped her bare, running their work-soiled hands over her until their pricks were rearing their heads furiously and I saw that Enid's nipples were stiffening too. The semen was overflowing from her and forming a sticky, drying trail down her thighs. From where I sat, I could smell her sex and it warmed me like a rich and costly wine, making me light-headed and filling my stones once more with seed that they longed to spurt forth on to the foul hussy's breasts and backside.

Aluf and Gunnar now laid Enid down on the rush-strewn floor and took turns. Her cries of fear and discomfort soon changed to the low moan of pleasure which I had too seldom heard from her when she lay in my bed; and it filled me with rage that I could not provoke such pleasure in her, whilst two filthy labourers could bring her to delight merely by flinging her upon the earth floor and violating her.

When they had done with her, and gone back to their work, leaving Enid panting on the floor, Hilde pulled her to her feet.

'No,' she rebuked her. 'You must not put your clothes back on. For there is yet one more task for you to perform, and you must perform it naked.'

Enid looked at her uncomprehendingly, no doubt beyond reason now.

'Take this basket,' Hilde commanded her. 'Go into the woods and gather kindling for the kitchen fire. Then return here. But remember this: if any man make demand of you, no matter how vile or depraved, you must allow him to have his will. And know this also: that there will be eyes upon you, and if you refuse any man his will, it shall be the worse for you when you return. Do you understand?'

Enid nodded silently, and took hold of the basket. With not so much as a backward glance at me, she opened the door and stepped out into the summer sunshine, her flesh gleaming white in the noonday heat.

I followed her at a distance, not wishing that she should see who was watching her. She walked across the fields towards the woods. To my disappointment, there seemed not a soul in sight to view my Lady Enid in all her naked glory, nor yet to demand the gift of her favours. Perhaps my ruse had not been so clever, after all. Mayhap I should have left her there in the kitchens, to take her chance with the pedlars and minstrels who came there nightly in the hope of lodging and other comforts.

But as I followed her deep into the woods. I saw a shadowy figure step out into the path, ahead of her. She gave a start, for it was the old hermit who had lived many years in a cave nearby, far from other men. For a moment, I felt keenly disappointed: after all, what carnal demands could an old hermit make upon a beautiful young woman like Enid? But I was to be surprised.

I hid behind a tree, and watched what next transpired.

'Good morrow, young woman,' the aged hermit hailed her.

'Good morrow, Brother,'

'Thou art indeed a comely wench,' said the hermit, gazing upon her loveliness wonderingly. He stretched out a wrinkled old hand and touched the tip of her breast. She shivered, I could not tell whether out of fear or appreciation. 'Comelier than I have seen these long years past. But tell me why thou art alone and naked in these woods, where so much danger lurks.'

'I am sent forth to gather kindling, Brother. And to bring comfort to any man who asks it of me.'

'Then will you offer me your comfort, wench? Will you come with me to my cell, where none can see?'

Incredulous, I followed Enid and the hermit further into the forest, until they reached the entrance to the old man's cave. When they entered, I followed and crept silently in behind them, hiding myself behind an outcrop of rock.

The cave was gloomily lit by a tallow candle which

cast an eerie glow around the bare walls. In the corner, a rough woollen blanket cast over a pile of dried bracken served as a bed. A wooden cross and a jug of water were the only other furnishings.

'Come in, my dear. Do not be afeared.'

'What would you have me do, Brother?'

'I would have thee kneel and perform thy devotions, child,' he replied, pulling his brown woollen habit over his head to reveal a surprisingly large and lively prick.

Enid obeyed, kneeling down on the cold earth floor. The hermit stood before her and placed his stones between her reverently clasped hands, gasping with pleasure as she opened her rosebud mouth and swallowed down his eager penis. She rubbed and stroked his stones, weighing them with all the reverent care of a novice bearing incense.

'No, no . . . Stop, child. You will provoke me too soon, bless you, child! Now pray you get down on all fours on the bed.'

Enid obeyed, her lovely arse displayed as she knelt with her knees apart on the bracken bed. The hermit knelt down behind her, and – clearly to her great surprise – set about lubricating her wrinkled arsehole with the love-juices which still flowed abundantly from her. She made no complaint as he pulled her bum-cheeks apart, aimed his manhood at the target and pressed home his advantage – though she must surely have suffered from so violent an assault upon her virgin hole.

The holy man rode her like an expert horseman, so furiously that her breasts bobbed about like delicious rosy apples, hanging juicily from some exotic tree. How I longed to pluck them, to sink my teeth into that sweet rosy flesh.

The hermit poured his seed into the Lady Enid's arse with a cry of triumph, and then withdrew quickly and dressed himself in his old brown robe.

'Yours is a fine charity, my wench,' he beamed, kissing Enid lightly on the cheek. 'Will you stay here with me this day, this night?'

'Alas no, Brother; for I have errands to perform, and must hurry back to my mistress,' replied Enid. And she turned and left the cave, heading – to my surprise – further into the forest.

I followed at a safe distance – or so I believed; watching to see where my wife Enid would lead me next. The afternoon was drawing on, and I began to worry. The woods were a dangerous place after nightfall, and I had brought neither sword nor armour to defend myself or the Lady Enid.

Watchful though I was, I was not prepared for what happened next. The branches of the trees suddenly came alive with armed men, leaping down and surrounding both myself and the Lady Enid. Outlaws! Masterless men who roamed the forests, killing and robbing and raping wherever they chose. And then, riding into the clearing on a fine white horse, came their leader, a tall young man, masked but clearly very fine-featured and dark; some young nobleman gone to the bad.

To my astonishment, the Lady Enid seemed not at all afraid. On the contrary, she ran forward to the masked horseman and held out her arms to him. He bent down and hoisted her on to his saddle so that she sat before him, radiant and smiling like some beautiful, unearthly goddess. The armed men drew closer around me, swords drawn; and I feared my time had come.

'No!' cried Enid, as they raised their swords to strike

me. 'Let him live. It is punishment enough that he should lose his wife to a band of brigands – the shame will be his reward for what he has done to me, to his faithful wife.'

'Faithful!' I cried, the rage almost choking me and making me forget all my fears. 'You are a faithless hussy, a strumpet, a jade, a whore who goes with any man who desires her. You deceived me whilst I was away in the Holy Land. And now you are running away from me with this band of filthy brigands. How can you tell me I have unjustly chided a faithful wife?'

'Know this, my husband Erek,' replied Enid, quietly but firmly. 'I never deceived you. Though I was sore tried during your long absence, and courted by many a handsome man, always I remembered you and resisted their advances. This man who holds me now paid his court to me, and I desired him dearly. But I sent him away, for I was a faithful wife to you.

'Late last night, the cook Hilde came to me and told me with what horrors you had planned to punish me for these imagined infidelities. And she and I plotted to rob you of your victory. She sent word to my lord the robber baron to meet me here in the forest, and so you see me now: faithless at last, but only because you constrained me to faithlessness.'

'But Enid . . . you are my wife! I loved you . . .!' I cried struggling to reach her, but thwarted by the armed cut-throats who hemmed me in on all sides.

'Such love it was that drove you to force me into the arms of other men!' she cried scornfully. 'And a cruel love indeed that takes its pleasure from seeing the mingled seed of other men cascading from my sex. Farewell cruel husband! You shall see me no more.'

And, turning his horse's head, the masked rider galloped away through the trees, with my naked wife before him. His henchmen bound me and knocked me senseless, leaving me to the mercy of the night beasts and vagabonds who roam the forests.

The following morning, Aluf and Gunnar found me and took me back to the manor. I sent out a search party to find Enid and her abductor; but by then they were far away.

And I never saw my wife again. Not to this very day.

Sir Galahad

A hush fell over the candle-lit hall as the knights considered in silence the terrible tale of Sir Erek and his virtuous wife. The veiled woman took her slender ringed hand from Erek's trembling shoulder, and he felt the power dissolving away, the spell losing its grip on him, the terrible compulsion ebbing, draining out of him. He took a long swig of wine from the drinking-horn and cast an uneasy glance at Arthur.

The King looked pale and shocked. What was going to happen next? Surely there could not be any more terrible secrets to be revealed? He could scarcely believe that his pure-hearted knights could have committed such acts of sexual barbarism – or that, having committed them, they could have brought themselves to confess them with such apparent fervour. He could only conclude that they were so doing in order to sacrifice themselves to the cruel, veiled sorceress and so save unwary Merlin from his captivity and Arthur's realm from terror and destruction.

The veiled figure drew all eyes. The ivory beauty of the woman's skin gleamed unearthly pale in the candles' glimmer, and her glorious nakedness inspired not only awe and terror but a ferocious tidal wave of lust, which washed over all who saw her. Her face was enticingly obscured by the heavy black veil, which trailed alluringly over creamy-white shoulders and threw the rounded perfection of her bosom into dazzling relief.

She walked twice more round the table, and the heady scent of her sex wafted intoxicatingly on the night air. Her excitement was growing. The game pleased her, and these tales of unworthiness were awakening her lust. As she passed by each knight, she let her cool white hand linger fleetingly on his hair, stroking slender fingers down his cheek and toying with his eager lips before passing on. The atmosphere was growing heavy with desire.

At last she halted, behind the chair of the purest knight of all, Sir Galahad. And she spoke, in the velvet tones of the heartless seductress:

'And so, my fine Sir Galahad, what of you? What tale have you to tell us, O purest and most chaste Knight of the Round Table? Can it be that you have nothing to offer me, nothing to reveal which might incline me to choose you over your fellows? Remember that the wizard Merlin's life depends upon your inventiveness.'

Galahad trembled inwardly, but raised his head boldly and replied.

'I have nothing to hide from you, and nothing to fear, evil sorceress. For I have led a pure and blameless life, as I shall now relate.'

He opened his mouth to speak, intending to tell a tale of purity and chivalrous chastity; but at that moment, he felt the touch of the veiled woman's hand upon his shoulder. It felt as though an icy wind were gusting through his very soul, destroying his will and taking away his power to resist her wishes. And at that same moment he felt her face draw down close to his own, the firmness of her cool, white breasts pressing into his back, and her icy breath on his cheek as she spoke to him once again:

'Alas, my poor knight; for you cannot resist my commands. Know that you are compelled by the power of my magic, and the magic of Merlin, to speak the truth.'

Then she drew herself up straight and spoke aloud:

'Speak, Sir Galahad. I grow weary, and time grows short, as you can see.'

And she raised her arms above her head, and as Galahad gazed before him he saw Merlin transformed into his future fate: a wizened husk of a man, with sunken eyes and hollowed cheekbones, slavering and crying out with the pain of his massively engorged prick, whose incessant demands he was now powerless to satisfy.

Trying desperately to resist, for he feared the shame and degradation his story would surely provoke, Galahad began to speak. But the words he meant to speak dried to dust in his throat, and the truth came tumbling forth.

THE TALE OF SIR GALAHAD
AND THE LADY AMIDE

It was late spring, and a beautiful morning when I rode forth from Camelot on the bidding of my liege lord, the King. I had heard that a beautiful maiden, the Lady Asphodel, had been taken against her will to a nunnery and imprisoned there on the command of her cruel aunt, a beautiful sorceress jealous of her niece's purity and budding beauty. Such a tale of distress sore wounded my pure heart, and I made great haste to the nunnery to rescue the damsel and restore her to her sweetheart.

It was nightfall when I reached the nunnery. The convent buildings were surrounded by a high wall, designed to keep prying eyes out and its secret treasures safe within, but I succeeded in climbing the wall and dropping down silently into the gardens below.

The gracious moon lit my pathway as I crept towards the door of the novices' dormitory, where I understood the Lady Asphodel was being held. It was unlocked, and I slipped easily inside, past the elderly nun who guarded the way and had fallen asleep at her post.

I found myself in a long corridor, with doors leading off it. The doors had small grilles, through which I was able to peer into the individual cells. Strange to tell, the flickering candlelight showed me that all were empty, the simple beds deserted – apparently in some haste. This seemed most strange to me, for it was not yet the hour of service, and all should have been soundly asleep.

As I walked further down the corridor, the strangest sounds came to my ears. I could have sworn I heard sighs and moaning, mingled with half-stifled laughter. Laughter! In this place of worship and sanctity! I hurried on, for I sensed at once that all was not as it should be.

At length, I came to the end of the corridor and a heavy wooden door. The sounds were louder now, and I felt that before I entered the room beyond, I must first gain some impression of the evils with which I must do battle. By luck, the door was unlocked and there was no key in the lock, so I was able to kneel and peer through the keyhole.

Alas, would that I could have been spared such a terrible sight! For this was no scene of quiet sanctity or innocent joy. I looked forth upon a scene of the next terrible debauchery.

The room was evidently the novices' warming-room, for it was full of young girls and there was a roaring fire in the hearth. All were naked, their still-uncut hair falling in gleaming cascades over their smooth shoulders and parting to reveal budding pink-tipped breasts. A shameful stirring within my loins bade me cease watching, yet I could not. An irresistible force I had never felt before was driving me on, compelling me to drink in what I saw.

Six girls were gathered in the centre of the room, where a seventh was lying naked on a straw mattress, moaning and sighing as though she were in great pain, or pleasure. She was a deliciously ripe young maiden, her body firm and juicy as a peach just before it falls from the tree, there to be devoured. She had a mane of glossy black hair and another glossy bush at the top of her thighs – a sight which I had never before witnessed for I am, as you know, vowed to celibacy and have a mortal terror of womankind.

Though deeply ashamed that I should be witness to such sights, I marvelled at the girl's satin-skinned perfection, at the rosebud tips of her exquisite breasts, which trembled as she sighed and writhed about on the mattress, and at the strangely glistening pinkness between her thighs. Overcome with a feeling I could not describe, I looked on, and my breathing grew heavy and an unaccustomed warmth and stiffness spread through my troubled loins.

The other six maidens were exploring her body now, teasing and titillating her with fingers and tongues; running their long hair over her skin and giggling with delight as they coaxed her pink nipples into stiffness. Now two of the maidens were holding the girl's thighs apart, and she was making a great show of resisting, of trying to pull away from them. But I could see from her face that she was a willing victim of these unspeakable outrages. And the pink-ness between her thighs was becoming a tide of wetness, making me yearn – I knew not why – to kiss it and drink down its honey-sweetness. I saw a little pink pearl glistening as it grew and swelled between her thighs, and heard the girl moaning and imploring:

'Touch me, I beg of you: lick me, take me, anything!'

One of the six girls, who had previously had her back to me, turned briefly to face me and my heart grew cold with fear and shame. For I found myself looking into the eyes of the Lady Asphodel, so recently a terror-stricken captive, and now – or so it seemed – apprenticed to the foulest perversities.

Asphodel was kneeling now, between the parted thighs of her victim. And I saw her put out her tongue and thrust it thirstily into the wetness offered to her. She circled the lips, lapping up the juices, and then began to lick away systematically at the little pink pearl. This seemed to please the girl very much indeed, for she began to moan and sigh more loudly than ever, and had to be silenced by one of the other girls thrusting a breast into her mouth to suck.

Meanwhile, the girls were toying both with their victim's breasts and with each other's. Asphodel was still lapping away at the girl's most intimate parts, and was now thrusting a finger inside her tight hole. Evidently this was a little painful – for the girl was yet a virgin and cried out as the finger slid into her – but she writhed enthusiastically upon this new toy, and was evidently most pleasured by it.

At that moment, I thought to enter the room and by force take away the Lady Asphodel from this den of vice. And yet the power of fascination held me still, and the yearnings I felt in my loin troubled my mind greatly, and seduced me to inaction.

As I was lamenting my own weakness of will, I saw a door open at the far end of the room. If I had expected the girls to make haste and rush back to their beds, as though nothing had happened, I was very much mistaken. For as a tall, robed figure entered the room, they looked up and smiled, and welcomed him in.

As the figure came into the centre of the room, the candleglow revealed him to me as a priest! My heart was sore troubled at such a terrible revelation. A man of the cloth, lending himself to such debauchery and corruption! I knew that I must immediately prevent events from proceeding any further and yet I could not. It is to my eternal shame and damnation that I continued there behind the door, watching and listening, and knowing nothing more than the dreadful torment of my loins, which distracted, bemused and yet delighted me in the strangest way.

The priest smiled and spoke:

'Good evening, my children. You have prepared yourselves well for the ceremony?'

'We have, Father,' they chorused reverently, their erect nipples very much at odds with their expressions of sanctity and respect.

'Whom have you prepared for me tonight, my child?' He addressed the Lady Asphodel, who sprang to her feet, her lips still moist with the juices from her ready victim.

'We have prepared the novice Gertrude,' replied Asphodel.

'Father, when will it be our turn to perform the ceremony with you?' asked a small, blonde girl with rounded hips and heavy breasts.

'Soon, soon, my child. Preparation is most important,' replied the priest indulgently. And by way of recompense for her disappointment, he bent and kissed the tips of her breasts, most gently and reverentially.

He now drew away and began to untie the knotted girdle about his waist. This he removed and handed to the blonde girl, who kissed it and ran it most charmingly across her creamy skin before laying it gently upon one of the beds.

The priest then lifted up the hem of his rough robe and pulled it over his head. He was naked underneath, and a fair sight. A young man, his body was firm and muscular, and I saw with amazement that from the base of his belly sprang forth a gnarled branch very much like the one I could feel sprouting and pulsating with sap in my own loins. His stones were large and well formed, contained within a loose, velvety pouch which tightened as his excitement grew.

He walked over to the girl and looked down at her, smiling with the satisfaction of one who is well pleased. She gazed up at him and reached up with her arms, stroking his legs and stretching up longingly towards his thighs and groin.

Obligingly, he knelt astride her chest, so that she

might better see and toy with these offerings which so delighted her. Groaning with pleasure and desire, she reached out and began to caress the priest's thighs, teasing the hairs with her small delicate fingers and running her index finger upward until it met the warm, moist crease that marks the division between leg and loins. She giggled delightedly as she caressed his stones and felt them tense up at her touch.

Then he took hold of her right hand and placed it upon his shaft, showing her how to work it up and down to give him pleasure and make it grow harder still. As I looked on, deeply ashamed of my own excitement, I envied him his boldness – for I knew that I could never have the courage to join my body to a woman's, and I have an abhorrence of self-abuse.

After a little while, he bade her stop, lest she bring him too far along the road to his pleasure. He got up and knelt between the girl's thighs, once more stimulating her to the limits of desire, with fingers and tongue.

At last he spoke:

'Are you ready to perform the ceremony, child?'

'Oh yes, Father, I am ready!'

'Hold her legs apart,' commanded the priest of the other girls. 'And suck at her breasts – it will render the ceremony more pleasurable and less painful for her.'

He then lay down upon her, placing the tip of his engorged organ against the coral-pink entrance to her secret cave. And with a mighty thrust, he ran her through. She gave a great cry – I know not whether of pain or of pleasure – but as soon as he began to ride her like a mare, she began to sigh and moan once again, urging him on:

'Faster, faster! Do it to me, Father! Make me a woman!'

And he obeyed her urgent pleas, thrusting into her flesh as lustily as any broadswordsman.

At last, he gave a final thrust, and they both cried out together as he fell forward upon her, her fingers clasped tightly to his buttocks, forcing him as far into her as he could go.

When he stood up, his organ was shrivelled and bloody, and the girl's thighs were running with red rivulets mingled with a pearly-white fluid which I guessed must have come from the priest's body.

The ceremony was over, and the priest dressed and left. As soon as he had gone, the girls put on their night-shifts and I realised that they were going to return to their cells. I hid myself and waited for them to pass, at last following the lovely, wicked Asphodel back to her cell.

I announced myself, and gave a respectful bow, never intimating any of the dreadful sights I had just seen:

'My lady, I have come to rescue you and take you to your lover, Sir Bedivere. I have come many miles on the bidding of my liege lord, King Arthur of Camelot. Will you haste away with me this night?'

The Lady Asphodel smiled demurely and nodded, kissing me very sweetly upon my cheek.

'At last you have come to rescue me!' she cried. 'And I have been languishing here for so long. I was sure that no one would come to save me, that I would surely die here, alone and unloved.'

For my part, I found it difficult to believe that this demure young damsel was that same shameless jade who had so readily participated in acts of the basest lust only moments earlier.

The maiden – or so I fervently hoped she still was – was clad in the purest white shift, and was modestly covered from neck to ankle. I could not drive from my mind the tormenting image of her naked body, of her smooth ivory back, or her creamy buttocks parting invitingly as she bent forward to lap at the moistness of her sister novice. Indeed, this image troubled me so greatly that I could scarce look the girl in the eye, and a terrible fear stole over me as she smiled invitingly at me.

I knew I must hurry her away from this place, or risk discovery and all that might entail. I bade her dress, turning my face to the wall as she clad herself in her novice's habit – the only clothes she now possessed – and trying not to listen to the seductive rustle of her night-shift as she pulled it over her head and cast it to the floor. Then, covering my turbulence as best I could, I took her by the arm and led her out of the convent, across the gardens and towards the high perimeter wall.

As I put my hands around her tiny waist to lift her to the top of the wall, her habit rode up and I caught sight of her beautiful, rounded buttocks beneath, naked and terrifying to my unpractised eye. The maiden was not slow in responding to what she no doubt believed to be an amorous advance; and she turned and smiled at me, sweetly and seductively.

'You have saved me, good Sir Knight. And you most assuredly have earned your reward. All that I have to give is yours – you have only to ask, to take.'

Hurriedly, I helped her over the wall, to the ground on the other side and on to the back of my waiting charger.

It was late, and the journey before us a long one. And so I took the girl to a manor house where we begged lodging for the night. An elderly serving woman took the girl away to the lady of the manor's private apartments, and I believed I was now safe from the damsel's amorous attentions.

Alas, in the small hours of the night, as I lay wrapped in my cloak on the straw in a barn, lodged with the humble beasts as is my preference, I felt the gentlest touch upon my brow: the touch of a pair of sweet lips, the touch of perfumed breath wafting across my cheek.

I opened my eyes and saw the Lady Asphodel looking down at me, smiling and stroking my face.

'What are you doing here, my lady? It is so late.'

'I have not yet thanked you properly for saving me, good Sir Knight. Surely you will not be so ungracious as to refuse my little gift of gratitude.'

I looked up at her in horror. Surely she would not risk her own and my reputation . . . Surely she would not . . .?

'My lady, you must return to your bed immediately. It is cold, and see – you are wearing only your night-shift.'

She seemed delighted at my solicitousness.

'It is indeed cold, my lord. But see: if you open up your big cloak it will serve to cover us both. And it is so much warmer to lie with another than to lie alone. Even the beasts lie together in pairs.'

'But madam!' I cried, as she pulled apart the edges of my cloak and, unfastening the tapes that held together her flimsy night-shift, she lay down beside me and pressed her nakedness against me.

Her knowing fingers caressed me in ways unimaginable, arousing me to a peak of sensation – and yet the terror that stole into my heart would not be stifled.

With a cry of terror, I pushed the maiden from me and called the serving woman to take her back to her room.

At first light, I escorted her to the house of her lover, Sir Bedivere, then rode away with all the haste I could muster.

I was greatly shaken by my experiences with the young lady Asphodel. For I had believed myself invulnerable to woman's charms, and there was terror in my heart, battling with the ferocious flames of my all-consuming lust. Yes, I cannot deny it. My heart was aflame with desires I had never before known, and I feared greatly for my purity.

And yet I truly believe I would have had the power to resist and to remain a pure and untainted knight, had I not angered the Lady Asphodel's aunt, the powerful sorceress. Though I knew it not, she knew that I had been the instrument of her niece's freedom, and even at that very moment she was plotting my downfall.

Unknowing, I made haste to return to Camelot, there to report upon the events which had befallen me, and to relate the tale of my temptation and how I had overcome it.

After a day's ride, I came to the little house which belongs to the mother of my fellow knight, Sir Perceval. The old woman was sitting outside her house, weeping, and being comforted to no avail by her friends and neighbours.

'What ails thee, my lady?' I cried, dismounting from my steed and hastening to her aid.

'Good Sir Knight; gentle Sir Galahad; how shall I be comforted? For my only daughter Amide has been stolen from me by a wicked sorceress, who has imprisoned her on a magic ship. None can rescue her, for only the pure in heart may cross the magical barrier which she has cast about the ship.

'And still worse! He who seeks to cross the threshold must come unarmoured and unarmed, protected by no sword or breastplate from the evil forces that await him. Through the purity of his own mind and body alone must he seek my daughter's salvation.'

My mind was in a turmoil; for the sweet lady Amide was known to me as not only the most beautiful of young women, but also the epitome of feminine chastity – pure and unsullied and a model for all her sex. I had long felt the most respectful affection towards this young lady, and I at once determined to rescue her.

'Fear not, my lady,' I cried. 'I shall return your daughter to you, unsullied and unharmed.'

It took two days and nights, without sleep, to reach the seashore where I had been told that my Lady Amide was held against her will. It was a sad and dull dawn, with a murky sky and a low, blood-red sun casting ghastly shadows upon the oily swell of the sea. At first, I saw no sign of any ship. The sea seemed bare of all life, from the shore to the horizon, and I began to believe that I had been tricked.

And then, lo and behold! As though from out of nowhere the graceful form of a golden sailing ship appeared before my eyes. 'Twas the most beautiful of vessels: entirely golden from stem to stern; its rigging of the finest gold thread, plaited and twisted into exquisite ropes. Its jewel-studded decks glittered more brightly than the very sun itself, and I was dazzled utterly.

Despite the sea-swell, the ship neither bucked nor rocked from side to side. It seemed to glide over the water, moving as fast and as smoothly as some strange seabird. And it slid towards the jetty on which I was standing, and came to a halt a few feet away from me, its golden sails shimmering in the early morning light.

A magic ship indeed. And I was sore afraid; but knowing that I was pure in heart and body, I cast off my armour, threw down my sword and stepped forth on to the deck with a brave heart, resolved to rescue the Lady Amide, no matter what dangers might befall me. Alas, for my poor pride.

As I stepped on to the deck, I felt a slight resistance, as though I were passing through an invisible wall, a cloak of magic protecting the ship from impure invaders. And then I was on the ship, and knew that I had passed the test of purity. Immediately I set about searching the ship for the captive Amide.

But scarcely had I begun to descend the steps into the bowels of the ship than I was thrown to the ground by a sudden violent motion of the ship. Clambering unsteadily to my feet, I looked about me and realised with horror that the ship was moving! It was speeding across the sea as fast as lightning, ten times faster than I had seen it moving before. And I looked out across the sea and saw strange shapes forming in the air. Strange shapes which troubled more than my mind.

I looked before me and saw a host of beautiful maidens, clad only in diaphanous veils of many hues. They were dark-haired and dark-eyed, full-bosomed and cherry-lipped, smiling at me and dancing sinuously in the air before my eyes.

'Galahad, Galahad,' they breathed, and their voices blended in an ethereal harmony which pierced my mind, my heart, my body, and made me tremble with an untold, undreamed-of desire.

'No, no!' I cried. 'You cannot harm me, for I am pure of mind and heart and body.'

'Galahad, sweet Sir Galahad,' they moaned, and their cries made me ache and turned my loins to fire. 'Will you not play with us, will you not dance with us?'

And the maidens began to disrobe before me, casting aside their veils until they were clad only in the swirling morning mists of the lowering cloudy air – wisps of grey and white and pink cloud, caressing their bodies, streaming across their full breasts, their swelling thighs, passing between their parted legs and making them sigh with the pleasure of the gentle touch.

Then three of the maidens came forward, so close to the ship that I feared they would touch me. But instead of doing so, they began to touch themselves lasciviously, pinching the tips of their breasts with crimson fingernails, passing a hand between their thighs, and all the time crooning to me soft and low:

'Galahad, Galahad, come to us, satisfy us! We are so hot and moist, and only for you. Only you can ease this aching. See! We are rubbing our clitties for you, sticking a finger into our hot holes, into our tight arses. How good it feels! How much better it would feel to have you inside us, sweet knight. Will you not fuck us? Will you not come inside us and spurt your beautiful white sperm into our bellies?'

'No, no!' I cried, and I fell to my knees on the deck, clasping my head in my hands and screwing my eyes tight shut, terror-stricken and desperate not to hear the seductive voices calling to me. But nothing would blot out their whispers, and soon I was compelled to part my fingers and peer through at the irresistible sight before my long-starved eyes.

'Galahad,' they whispered; and I could almost feel their hot breath on my cheek, their skilful fingers easing away my clothes. 'We know how much you want us, desire us, need us. We know your cock is rearing its impudent head inside your hose.'

'But I am sworn to chastity!' I sobbed. 'None shall sully the pure body of Sir Galahad!'

'But how can it be right for a fine young knight to forswear the company of beautiful damsels such as we?' they pleaded, cupping their delectable breasts in their hands and offering them to me as though they were some rare and exotic sweetmeat. 'Take, eat . . . These are our bodies,' they smiled, in a hideous parody of the Sacrament of Holy Communion. 'Do you not hunger, do you not thirst? Do you not yearn for the ripeness of woman's flesh?'

And I howled out my distress, for it was true: my own flesh was yearning for conjunction and consummation, and my manhood strained painfully within my hose.

As I watched, the damsels began to touch each other, to cause each other such wanton delight that I felt a strange dampness moistening the tip of my eager manhood, in spite of my terror. They adorned each other's bodies with shameless kisses and intimate caresses, and I saw the juices running down their thighs as their sexual parts opened like exotic blossoms to release their fragrant tide of nectar.

And then, just as I was convinced that I could bear no more and must surely weaken or perish for my purity, I looked up and saw that my tormentors were gone.

Still shaking, I stood up and made my way unsteadily down the steps into the depths of the vessel. I found myself in a wondrous golden saloon, richly decorated with gold leaf carvings and solid gold ornaments, and lit by shimmering candles in a golden chandelier.

On a table in the middle of the saloon was laid out food and drink in golden dishes and goblets – a lavish banquet for one. Although my better judgement told me not to taste any of this magic bounty, a strange thirst stole over me and I found my throat so dry that I rashly drank down a goblet of wine. It was rich and red and sweet, and as it slid down my throat I felt its hidden potency entering the very heart of me. A warmth spread through my body, and my manhood stiffened anew, tormenting me with fresh desires I had no means to satisfy.

I looked down and saw that a sheet of gold-edged parchment had mysteriously appeared on the table. I picked it up and as I looked at it, golden writing began to thread its way across the page. It read: 'WHAT YOU SEEK YOU WILL FIND IN THE CHAMBER OF DIAMONDS AND RUBIES'.

It was then that I realised, with shame, that in my own torment I had almost forgotten what I had come to seek: the deliverance of the Lady Amide from her terrible captivity. At once I resolved that I must find and rescue her.

Each of the rooms leading off the saloon was decorated in different precious gems: the first in emeralds, the second in amethysts, and the third in sapphires. But all were empty. I opened the final door and was greeted by a dazzling flash of red and sparkling white fire: this, at last, must be the chamber of diamonds and rubies.

As my eyes became accustomed to the light, I saw a golden bed in the centre of the chamber, and on it, the slender figure of a young woman, wrapped in a white shroud. Alas! Could it be that the Lady Amide was already dead, and that I had been brought here only to weep at her deathbed and bear back the news of her sad fate to her mother and brother?

I looked down at her and recognised the sweet face of the Lady Amide, the dark, tumbling locks and ivory skin. I could scarce believe her dead, though her eyes were closed, for there was a flush of pink in her cheeks and her lips were full and crimson-red. I bent down and placed a reverent kiss upon those glossy lips, little guessing what would then follow.

For as my lips touched hers, Amide's eyelids shot open and I found myself gazing into her eyes of brilliant blue. She was alive! Why then did she not speak, not move, not show me some sign?'

Perhaps her movements were impeded by the tightness of the winding-sheet about her fragile limbs. I must free her body from its prison, and warm some life back into her lifeless frame.

I at once set to work upon the poor maiden's almost lifeless body.

At first I worked but slowly at the fabric of the shroud, but as it rolled back to reveal the curves of the damsel's body, I began to work more quickly, the strange fire in my loins responding like quick-silver to the beautiful sight now revealed to my eager eyes.

As the last fold of the shroud fell away, I gave a gasp of sudden joy to see the perfection of her young, now sadly powerless body. This was indeed perfection. Slender, yet rounded, with swelling hips and breasts as succulent and inviting as ripe exotic fruit. A dream of joy, and yet a torment for one such as I, vowed unto celibacy.

Amide looked up at me desperately – could it be that she was begging me to bring life to her paralysed frame? She was evidently quite incapable of any movement. Perhaps if I were to rub her limbs a little, that would bring the life blood back to them?

Gingerly at first, I placed my hand upon her arm and began to caress it. Amide gave a little gasp, and began to breathe a little faster. I took this as a sign of encouragement, and began to rub harder. I noticed that her pink rosebud nipples were beginning to stiffen, and felt that this must be a sign of some success.

Then I moved my hands to her legs, caressing them tenderly from feet to thighs, and all the time telling myself that all that I was doing was out of a spirit of Christian charity. And all the time, the warmth in my loins was spreading, my stones tensing and an overwhelming compulsion driving me on to other, less modest embraces.

'O lovely Amide,' I entreated her. 'Is it true that you can neither speak nor move? Answer me with your eyes if you cannot speak.'

And in answer, she closed her lovely blue eyes once, a tiny tear appearing at the corner of her eye. I kissed it away, and as I leant forward to plant my lips on her face, I felt the hard tips of her breasts burrowing into my flesh.

A thought came to me:

'Can you then feel my touch upon you? Close your eyes once if you can feel me.'

And she closed her beautiful eyes once again, and I trembled to think of the power which Heaven had bestowed upon me.

For the first time, I had before me a naked and beautiful woman, a maiden pure of heart and body, and powerless to exert any wiles upon me, powerless either to resist me or to overwhelm me with knowing lust, as might so many wicked and impure women. I felt my own body responding as it had never done before; surely, then, this must be a Heavenly command, an obligation placed upon me? For how could it be wrong for the act to be committed between two pure souls? And had not Amide's mother told me that I must save her daughter through the purity of my mind and body? Alas, the voice of evil spoke seductive words in my ear.

My hands began to rove across Amide's perfect skin, full of the wonderment of new discovery. Wondrous folds and furrows of sweet flesh, untouched and undefiled, for my unpractised fingers to explore. Oh, what sweet palaces and groves to wander through! See: here are twin fruits that seem ready to burst with sap as I caress them and they grow harder, rosier, riper to the touch. Their little stalks are hard and so sweet to the taste – here, let me pluck a fruit and savour its fragrance, its texture in my mouth. And here: a smooth and silky plain that slopes down gently until it reaches the sweetest little thicket of soft foliage. Feel my fingers, Amide: feel them exploring, entwining, delighting in this scented verdure. For I bring my face close to the grassy triangle, and breathe in a heady fragrance which bewitches my senses and makes my head spin. I have almost forgotten why I am doing this . . . Almost forgotten that I have taken a sacred vow . . .

There was an unbearably heavy sensation in my loins, a weight of pleasurable pain in my stones, that felt like fruits so ripe they would surely burst their skins and pour forth their juice upon the fertile earth of Amide's belly and bosom. My remaining clothes were unbearably burdensome to me, and I quickly stripped off my shirt and hose, freeing my burgeoning manhood which – to my amazement – I found myself caressing with every bit as much diligence as I was using to caress the lovely Amide's nakedness.

The glistening purple head of my manhood slid deliciously between my fingers as I worked the shaft slowly up and down, and a glistening bead of clear fluid appeared at the little eye in its very tip. I touched it wonderingly, and found it slipped delightfully between finger and thumb. Pleasure mounted in my balls and I felt an unbelievably strong urge to pump faster, to allow myself to be borne away upon the swelling tide which I did not yet understand, and yet could feel rising up within my loins. I sensed that a new and very wonderful pleasure would be gifted to me if I would only give way to its seductive power.

And yet a voice within me told me I must not give way to such guilty pleasure. I must remember my divine mission: to use what the good Lord had provided as the means of salvation for my poor Lady Amide, lying there helpless before me, her breath still quickening, and her beautiful blue eyes moist with tears.

With a terrible reluctance, I let go of my engorged manhood and let it spring back against my belly, magnificent in its power and readiness: a worthy weapon, or so I believed, for a pure-hearted knight who is about the work of the Lord.

I turned my attentions once more to Amide, and as I began to caress her nipples and breasts I saw her gaze soften – I believed with yearnings which I, too, felt acutely within my loins. Moving from her stiffening nipples, I explored her softly rounded belly and swelling hips, sliding my hands beneath her to knead her cool white buttocks and venture a little further into that dark and secret furrow that lay between them. I delighted in the way her tight little nether hole twitched in response as I gently stroked it with my fingertips; then I brought my hands back round her hips and began to attend once more to my lady's belly and thighs.

Such beauty I had never seen before, much less had I ever touched or thought to enjoy. For I had forsworn all fleshly pleasures. At last, I was to enjoy the delights of womanhood and yet not sacrifice my purity – what joy! Or so I fondly believed.

I stroked Amide's dark curly triangle once again, and a tiny gasp from Amide reassured me that I had chosen a wise pathway. I ran my fingers up her thighs and then, a little bolder, began to insinuate them in between. It was not an easy task, for my lady's body was quite motionless and the lady helpless either to assist or resist me. Alas, for I believed the tears in her eyes were tears of gratitude . . .

With a little force, I succeeded in pulling Amide's thighs apart, parting her legs so that the beautiful musky scent of her most intimate and womanly parts wafted up like incense from a blessed chapel. And I was her worshipper, quite, quite bewitched as I bowed my head in the greatest reverence and began to explore her with my lips and tongue.

Her scent was heavy and her essence sweet and abundant. Nuzzling my face between her thighs, I pulled apart her nether lips with eager but gentle fingers, as one might separate the petals of a rare blossom, the better to sip at its nectar. I was amazed by the beauty of what I saw, spread out before me: a fur-trimmed casket of precious delights, and at their very heart, a glistening pink pearl which seemed to grow and swell even as I looked at it.

Wonderingly, I extended my tongue and lapped at the little pink rosebud. Immediately a flood of the sweetest dew anointed the rosebud and refreshed my parched tongue. Eager to seek the source of such wondrous refreshment, I wriggled a finger inside the moist pink tunnel. I was excited beyond belief to feel the fleshy obstruction barring my way, for I knew that this frail partition must be the token of my lady's jealously guarded chastity, that most precious treasure of all: her maidenhead.

At the sudden thought that it was I, Galahad, who had been chosen from all men as the only one pure enough to relieve my lady of her maidenhead, my prick leapt more stiffly still to attention and begged to bury itself within the inert body of my lady Amide. And how should I deny her the sacred unction, which I felt sure, was the only means by which I could restore to her the power of grace and motion?

In a sudden surge of spiritual elevation, I fell upon the maiden and sought to make an entrance into her inner temple. Alas, so ill experienced was I that my first attempt ended in failure. But, clasping tight hold of her creamy thighs, I placed the tip of my lance against her glistening entrance, and pressed home my advantage. Though forceful and zealous, my thrust was impeded by the maiden's curtain of virtue, which, frail as it seemed, resisted me almost to the last. But, with a final thrust, I forced my way through the gates of her maidenhead and joined her own purity to my own.

The sensations which flooded me were so exquisite that I believed I must surely be glimpsing Heaven and the Holy Grail. For my loins were bathed in the most delicious warmth which began to spread through my entire body. The poor Lady Amide lay motionless and almost silent beneath me, but tears were streaming down her lovely face and I swear I began to feel my own body's warmth transmitting itself to her cold and lifeless limbs. Certain now that I had not been mistaken, I thrust home again and again, joining this most divine purpose to my celestial pleasure.

Her tunnel was warm and welcoming, tight as a hand about my manhood, yet moist and silky-smooth, bathing me with the juices of Amide's arousal. Waves of pleasure crashed upon a distant shore, and I forgot that she and I were prisoner upon a strange and magical vessel, that we might never more see land, that we might both have been lured into a trap which would hold us for eternity. My only thought now was to climb up to the summit of joy and take her with me.

With a cry of ecstasy – the first in my young life – I reached the summit of the mountain and stepped into the cool, clear air of purest pleasure, tumbling down through sunlit skies until at last I fell, panting and sated, upon the breast of my lovely Amide. And as I cried out, Amide joined her cries to mine, and oh joy! I felt her hands fluttering into life and clasping my buttocks, pulling me deeper into her. I felt her thighs warming, moistening, tightening about my own.

We lay together for a few moments, panting and bedazzled by the moments we had just shared.

And then Amide raised herself on one elbow and struck me hard across the face:

'Foolish knight, that hast robbed me of my maiden-head and thyself of thine own! You have forsaken the ways of virtue, and brought us both to the eternal damnation of guilty pleasure!' The tears were coursing down her face and she was sobbing. 'Do you not see that you have fallen into the trap laid by the sorceress who abducted me? She has lured you here and you have dishonoured us both.'

'But, my Lady Amide . . . Have I not restored to you the power of your most beautiful body, through the sacred joining of our pure bodies?'

At this, the Lady Amide fell a-sobbing on the bed and would not be consoled. And I began to doubt my own sanity.

Suddenly, the candle flames guttered and the room was plunged into darkness. I reached out for some object to use as a weapon, but I was powerless to defend myself or the Lady Amide since I could see nothing around or before me. A sudden blinding light made me cover my eyes in pain; and when at last I opened them, I saw before me a tall, dark-haired woman, dressed all in silver-spangled black.

' 'Tis the sorceress!' breathed Amide, trying in vain to hide her face from the apparition.

'Aye, my little lady,' replied the woman, with a laugh as hollow and humourless as a dry-boned coffin. 'What – proud no longer? Where is all thy proud virtue now? Hast thou discovered at last the joys of carnal sin? Well may you hide your face, hussy!'

Then she turned her face to me:

'Sir Galahad, pure Knight of the Round Table!' She flung back her head and laughed, her shoulders heaving with the mirth of it, and her generous breasts pressing against the thin fabric of her robe so that, despite my sudden shame, I felt a new stirring in my defiled loins. 'Pure no longer, my fine young sir! It was a good jest, worth the loss of my wayward niece Asphodel.'

'Foul fiend!' I cried, making as though to stroke her, then staying my hand – for I could not in all honesty strike down a woman, no matter how evil she might be.

'You cannot harm me,' she smiled. 'You are but a pretty toy and now you have outlived your usefulness.'

And with that, she lifted her arms and uttered words of power which plunged the room once more into utter blackness. The ship seemed to be spinning wildly and I fell to the ground, dazed and sick, unable to stand. Terrible images of naked women filled my head, my sight, their voices tormenting me, until at last I fell into a deep trance, and knew no more.

When I awoke, the ship and the Lady Amide had disappeared, I know not where, and I lay naked on a deserted shore, cold and alone. To this day, I know not how the lady reached home, but after many weary days I reached her mother's house, and discovered her there, pale and silent but seemingly well. To this very day, she has never told anyone what befell her on the magic ship; and until this fateful night I thanked Heaven that she had never revealed the shame of my defilement.

I stand before you now, no longer Galahad the Pure, but Galahad the Vile, the Unclean, the Libidinous.

His story done, the knight slumped forward, his head in his hands, and a ripple of astonishment ran round his companions at the table.

'Well told, Sir Knight,' breathed the veiled seductress, removing her hand from his shoulder. 'Perhaps you shall suffer yet more before this night is done. For I think that it would please me to see such purity further ravaged and defiled.'

Sir Alisander Le Orphelin

*T*here was a hush of expectation in the candle-lit hall. The boars'-head trophies which gazed sightlessly from the cold stone walls seemed now to see beyond the confines of time and space and into the hearts of the assembled knights. Hearts which had seemed so pure, so chivalric, now shown to be as base and despicable as the hearts of their enemies. Would there be none amongst the Knights of the Round Table worthy to bear the title? And, as each new story outdid the last in depravity, which of the knights would be chosen by the evil sorceress to become her doomed consort, her sexual prey?

All eyes turned from the hapless, downcast Galahad to the veiled sorceress, who was still shaking with silent laughter. At last she spoke:

'Sir Galahad, your own shame is truly punishment enough for such an ignoble deed. For how are the mighty fallen! The heart of the purest and most chaste Knight of the Round Table, laid bare before all your fellows and revealed as the hollow sham that it is!

However noble you imagined your motives to be, you have behaved basely. In allowing magic to dupe you and lust to guide you, you have deflowered the pure sister of an honourable knight, and now you shall never be worthy of the Grail quest.'

The sorceress gave a little laugh of satisfaction as she raised her ringed hand and pointed at unhappy Sir Galahad:

'Sir Knight, I can think of no worse torment for you than to condemn you to the constant memory of how you have fallen.'

Galahad hung his head in shame and began to sob into his hands with the terrible memory of what he had done, how he had discovered the lustful self which lurked beneath the surface of his piety, and how he had given in to the all-too-human side of his nature.

'And now let us turn to good Sir Alisander,' continued the sorceress, turning her gaze to the dark-haired knight who sat on the left hand of Sir Galahad. 'Sir Alisander Le Orphelin, what tale have you to tell us?'

And she laid her hand upon his shoulder and Alisander knew that, whatever he had hoped to say in his glory or defence, he must now tell the truth.

THE TALE OF ALISANDER LE ORPHELIN

I was born in a small manor in Brittany, the bastard son of the Comte de Vannes and his wife's maid, Agnes. My mother died at my birth and I was orphaned in infancy when my father was killed in battle. I was sent to the castle of my uncle, the Duc de Montrechatte, there to be brought up in the ways of the nobility – for the Duc had no son, and was desirous of an heir.

It was when I was only seven years old, and learning the duties of a squire, that I first realised my talent for moving about the castle unseen and unnoticed. For I had a light step and a quick eye, and knew all the secret ways.

One morning, the Duc called me into his apartments and bade me bear a message to one of the wenches who worked in the castle kitchens and who served at the Duc's table whenever it pleased him to see a pretty face and a well-turned ankle. For the Duc and Duchesse had lived separate lives these many years, and from time to time he felt the need of feminine company.

In my innocence, I imagined that the Duc wished for the wench to come to his apartments to clean them, or for some equally innocent purpose.

The wench Rosilde was a comely lass – a Norman farmer's daughter, purchased by the Duc from her father on a whim and brought to Brittany to serve him. She was generously made, as are all Norman wenches: she had a fine, strong-limbed body and broad hips, tapering to a surprisingly slender waist. Her arms rippled with muscles from all the fetching and carrying that was required of her. And I shall never forget her open, rosy-cheeked face topped with a straw-coloured mane of hair.

But most memorable of all was Rosilde's magnificent, friendly bosom. How many blissful hours I spent as a small boy, my sobs comforted as she pillowed my troubled head between her big, soft breasts. They were as soft as clouds, and as all-enveloping as a duck-down quilt; and many was the time I feigned sleep, so that she would not prise me from my soft and strangely exciting resting-place.

Rosilde was in the dairy, churning butter. As she turned the handle on the barrel, her muscles flexed and her big, soft bosom wobbled deliciously. How I longed for her to gather me up in her arms and press me close to those downy-soft breasts. And how I wished I could understand the strange emotions which raced through me as I imagined what those breasts would look like were she unclothed.

On seeing me, Rosilde smiled and bobbed a little curtsey.

'Good morrow, young master. Hast come to help me with the dairying?' For it was true that I spent much of my free time in the dairy, helping with small tasks so that I could be near the object of my fascination.

'Not today, Rosilde. My lord the Duc bids you come to his chamber.'

'And must I come now?'

'Oh yes, Rosilde. He told me that he has a most urgent need of your services.'

At these words, innocently issuing forth from the mouth of a mere babe, a broad smile spread across Rosilde's cheerful face.

'Then I must away immediately! Come – help me take off this apron.'

Eagerly I fumbled with the strings that held on her apron, revelling in the mingled scents of warm milk and sweat and – though I knew it not – ripe, luscious womanhood. She bent forward to place the apron on a bench, and her breasts hung for an instant like overripe fruit, so full of juice that it must surely burst forth in an inundation of sweetness.

Rosilde and I made our way quickly to the Duc's

apartments. She knocked upon the door, and a voice inside called out:

'Enter.'

She slipped inside and the heavy door closed behind her. I knew that I ought to tiptoe away and leave Rosilde and the Duc to whatever business they had to contract. But something inside me made me linger awhile; made me bend to peer through the keyhole.

It was quite dark inside the tower chamber, for the windows were no more than narrow slits in the thick stone walls; and it took a little time for my eyes to become accustomed to the gloom. When at last they did, I started with amazement at what I saw.

My dear friend Rosilde was stripped to the waist, her blouse lying discarded on the floor and her shift hanging down about her hips. The sight troubled me in ways which I was then, alas, too young to understand. Her breasts were even more beautiful unclad than I could have imagined them to be: huge, creamy-white pillows of flesh, crested with upturned pink stalks which, even as I watched, seemed to grow longer and pinker.

She was holding a discipline, similar to those which I had seen monks and pilgrims using at the annual Pardons to chastise their flesh. Rosilde was wielding the discipline with all the zeal of a penitent, and the exertion was both reddening her cheeks and making her flesh tremble delightfully.

But the greatest surprise of all was that she was not wielding the lash upon herself, but upon the naked, cowering figure of my lord the Duc! His bare back was already criss-crossed with angry red lines, and with each new stroke, the leather thongs bit new grooves into the martyred flesh. And at each stroke, the beautiful Rosilde's massive pillowy breasts bounced up and down, and how I longed to touch and stroke them! Why, I began to believe that even I might be willing to be beaten – if the beating was to be administered by Rosilde, and if she would undertake to comfort me afterwards and kiss the pain from my wounds.

Child that I was, I could not for the life of me comprehend why my lord the Duc should submit himself so humbly to a common serving wench – however comely – and allow her to beat him till his flesh was raw. And his cries as the lash fell on his back: terrible cries that were half of pain, half of some other emotion I scarcely understood. But I sensed that, in some strange way, the Duc was finding pleasure in his pain.

After a while, it seemed that Rosilde grew weary of her chastisement, for she left off beating the hapless Duc and, no doubt tired and hot after her exertions, set about removing the rest of her clothes.

My eyes were almost starting from their sockets as she unfastened her skirt and let it, and her shift, fall to the ground. As she stepped out of the clothes, I saw that she was entirely naked beneath her shift; and I saw her large rounded backside – two broad, dimpled cheeks like leavened dough, inviting the watcher to touch, stroke, knead.

She bent down and helped the Duc to his feet. He seemed shaky and had to hold on to her for support. But as he turned to face the door, I saw that one portion of his anatomy at least was lively and vigorous and as eager as you could imagine. I saw with amazement that my lord the Duc had a pizzle as I did; but that it was not made like mine: for instead of hanging limply between his thighs, my lord's pizzle was stiffly upstanding, its glistening purple head merrily dancing as the mighty instrument strained to grow even stiffer, even longer.

At that moment, the Duc recovered his forces quite miraculously, and began to kiss and caress sweet Rosilde as though he were deeply grateful to her for inflicting such horrible torment upon his flesh. She in turn responded with gentle caresses, very different in character from the harsh way in which she had lashed his back only minutes before.

She ran her work-callused hands over his flabby belly, and down into the thick grey-black bush out of which sprang the Duc's mighty staff. And she began to toy with it, which evidently gave the Duc great pleasure, for he began to groan quietly and pulled the wench closer to him, bending his head to take one of the long, pink nipples into his mouth and sucking as greedily as any hungry babe.

Then, to my bafflement, the Duc pulled the wench Rosilde over to his great curtained bed and pushed her so that she fell back on to it. She seemed not to mind this indignity, for I distinctly heard her giggling as the Duc lay on top of her, his red-streaked back and backside moving up and down.

I knew not what they were doing, so innocent was I. But a great confusion spread over me, and I blushed crimson to the roots of my hair as I watched the Duc and Rosilde frolicking within the Duc's chamber.

At that moment, I heard footsteps on the stair, and had to hurry away, back to my duties, still wondering at what I had seen and what meaning there could be in it. Still wondering at the great turmoil which had been wrought within me by the sight of Rosilde's glorious naked bubbies, bouncing and quivering upon her chest.

I never forgot Rosilde, or her wonderful nakedness. And I often thought back to that day, in my boyhood, when I had first discovered the delights of the voyeur, the unseen watcher who tastes the sweets of other men's clandestine passions.

On my sixteenth birthday, I was dubbed a squire to Sir Geraint, and came with him to Camelot, there to learn the ways of chivalry and to prepare myself for admittance to the ranks of the Knights of the Round Table.

I was a shy lad, not given to carousing or to disporting myself with women, though there were others of my age who had known women and boasted about it to me at night in the dark of the stables where we lowly squires slept. I often wondered what it would be like to touch and taste a woman's flesh; to slide my hand inside her shift, and feel the warm softness of her breasts, hard-nippled and ready for passion. The other lads had told me what happens between a man and a woman in the bedchamber, and I wondered how it would feel to slide my hard prick into a woman's wet hole, how it would feel as I exploded within her.

Already I had discovered the pleasures of self-abuse. And from time to time, in the darkness and privacy of our stable beds, we lads would play pretty games with each other's most intimate parts, delighted to see which of us would rise first to attention, and which would first send his foaming seed spurting out on to the straw with a long groan of pleasure.

But, pleasant as these distractions undoubtedly were, they could not satisfy my urge to experience a woman's flesh. And yet, I was too shy, too wary to put myself forward, though there were young girls aplenty for me to choose from – and wet and willing every one of them, if what my friends told me was true; but in truth, it was not the slender, pert-breasted young girls who most appealed to me, pretty sight though they were. I remembered plump Rosilde with her heavy, fertile hips and softly swelling breasts, and knew that this was what I most desired. To be enveloped and overwhelmed by a fine, strong woman like Rosilde.

Since I would not stoop to couple with a young wench, I must needs abstain, and my trusty fingers – and those of my kind friends – were my only comfort in those dark days and nights.

But my desire mounted. And one day, I was given an opportunity to fulfil my desire, at least in part.

Sir Geraint called me to him, and charged me take a message to his true love, the Lady Estella:

'You are a quiet and discreet lad,' he told me. 'I know that you will exercise utmost tact in all your master's commissions. Know you the Lady Estella?'

'I do, sir.'

'Then you will know that she is married to the Flemish knight Sir Baldwin of Ghent, who was badly wounded fighting in the Holy Land, and who can no longer satisfy her needs. She has turned to me in her hour of need, and how can I – chivalrous knight that I am – deny her the comfort which I alone can afford?'

There was a wicked twinkle in his eye; and I sensed that his motives were rather less honourable than he led me to believe. What is more, I comprehended instantly the need for secrecy. For the Lady Estella must not be dishonoured by any careless discovery of her liaison with Sir Geraint.

'I understand, Sir Geraint,' I assured him. 'What would you have me do?'

He produced a ring from his pocket, and handed it to me.

'Take this to the Lady Estella. Her manor is but a few hours' ride from here. It is a sign between us: when she receives the ring, she will know that it is safe to come to our meeting-place in the huntsman's lodge in Logres forest. Escort milady to the lodge – you know the place, for you have hunted with me there many times – and I shall greet her there. You may then await the lady's return.'

I bowed my assent and set off immediately for the Lady Estella's manor, some few leagues from Camelot. It was a rich manor, with a fine stone-built house and many outbuildings. I dismounted from my horse and entered the house, there to be greeted by an old woman dressed from head to toe in drab black.

'The master cannot see anyone,' she warned me. 'For he is sick and confined to his apartments.'

'I come with a message for the Lady Estella,' I explained.

The old crone shuffled off to find her, and a few moments later she arrived. She was not at all what I had expected. For most fine high-born ladies are slender as a willow, wan, pale and sickly looking. But the Lady Estella was tall and generously built, with a magnificent bosom that swayed delightfully as she walked. I could understand only too well how Sir Geraint had been tempted and enchanted by her, and why such a fine-looking woman could feel neglected in the time of her husband's indisposition.

I gave the Lady Estella the ring, and she smiled and told her maid to bring cloak and riding gloves.

'I am summoned by the Mother Superior to visit the Holy Sisters at the forest priory of Dene,' she announced. 'This young squire has kindly agreed to escort me. I shall be back late tonight.'

We rode in silence for most of the journey. For, although the Lady Estella seemed willing to talk, I found myself hopelessly tongue-tied in her presence. Her glorious womanly beauty quite overwhelmed me, and I knew that I should never have the courage to approach one such as she and confess my hidden, shameful desires.

The hunting lodge was a low wooden building almost hidden by the trees, and seldom visited by any save the knights of Camelot, when out on their hunting parties. It was the perfect setting for any clandestine meeting of lovers.

I saw with a keen sense of disappointment that Sir Geraint's horse was already tethered outside the hut. I had hoped to spend longer in the lady's company, for already her comely body had enchanted me.

Sir Geraint must have been watching for our approach, for the door swung open and he came out to greet Lady Estella, kissing her most gallantly and chastely upon the hand. He then turned to me:

'You have performed your duties well, my boy. Now, I bid you ride out to the fringes of the forest and wait for me in the hamlet of Redesford. I shall bring the Lady Estella to you before dusk, and you shall ride with her back to the manor this night.'

Although I had known he must surely send me back to Redesford, I was resentful of this prompt dismissal. But, with a heavy heart, I mounted my horse and rode away, towards the edge of the forest. As I left, I looked back over my shoulder and saw the two lovers go into the hut and close the door behind them.

But I did not ride out of the forest and back to

Redesford. I halted awhile, just out of sight of the lodge, for a wicked idea had entered my head. I remained where I was for a few moments, until I was sure that the lovers would be engrossed in each other, and too preoccupied to notice my return; then I dismounted, tethered my horse, and walked quietly back towards the lodge, being careful to take a back route which would ensure that they did not see my approach.

The lodge had few windows, and I saw that they were covered up with pieces of rough sackcloth, to keep out the cold air and give the occupants some privacy. This came as a blow to me, for if I pulled aside the sacking, Sir Geraint and his love would surely see me.

But I was in luck. For as I walked round the outside of the lodge, I saw that one of the pieces of sacking had a small hole in it, just big enough for me to place my eye against it and look through, into the cottage.

I tiptoed to the window, and bent to look through the hole. The afternoon sunlight was filtering into the lodge through the sackcloth, and the room inside was bathed in a sort of dull golden haze. The room was bare, save for a rough table and stool, a few cooking pots and snares, and a large pile of animal pelts which no doubt served the huntsman as a bed.

This was certainly how it was serving today. For the lovers were already naked and intertwined upon the soft fur bed. The Lady Estella was lying on her back, with her legs wide apart and her hands resting like a priest's upon the head of Sir Geraint, who was reverently kneeling between her thighs, his head bowed and buried in the dark thicket of her pubic curls.

Estella charmed me even more in her shameless

nakedness than she had done within the confines of her close-fitting velvet gown. Her large and shapely breasts stood out proudly and I imagined my head nesting between them, my lips closing around a puckered brown nipple and my tongue teasing it into willing rigidity. I dreamed myself a tiny and helpless babe, clutched to that mighty bosom, swimming in an ocean of sweet milk, floating on the clouds of those soft and ample breasts.

An intensely pleasurable warmth was spreading through my loins. Instinctively, I touched the front of my hose and felt a growing, pulsating staff of flesh which sought to escape from its prison and seek its home, its goal. Hungrily, I reached into my hose and wrapped my fingers around it, breathing more heavily as I felt the delicious touch of the engorged flesh. Quickly I pulled down the front of my hose and freed my prick. It was magnificently erect and stiffened still more as I peered through the hole into the room beyond.

With a piercing cry, my Lady Estella began to twist and turn and writhe upon the makeshift bed, her eyes rolling in their sockets. And I thought for a moment that she was in the throes of some dreadful seizure, or that she had been possessed by demons. But then she fell back on to the fur bed, panting heavily and with such a peaceful smile upon her face that I wondered if she had seen the faces of the angels.

When Sir Geraint raised his head from his devotions, my Lady Estella's most intimate parts were revealed for the first time to my unpractised gaze – and in truth this was the first time that I had ever made such an intimate acquaintance of any woman. 'Twas a wondrous sight indeed; my lady's hidden crack, opened up to receive her lover's attentions, and now unwittingly exposed to me as well as I stroked my throbbing shaft outside the window.

Her exposed flesh was so pink and moist I might have believed I was gazing upon some lively and appetising shellfish, running with delicious juice. How I longed to put out my thirsty tongue, and lap up those juices, let them roll over my tongue, flood my mouth and trickle in warm rivulets down my throat.

Now the tables were turned. Sir Geraint was lying on his back on the pile of furs, a saintly fellow with his pilgrim's staff at the ready, pointing ever-heaven-wards. His stones were taut and firm, and a bead of love-essence glistened at the tip of his shaft. The Lady Estella was now the supplicant at the altar, kneeling between her lover's thighs and bowing low to make her plea; her lips opening and closing about his staff in the tenderest of prayers.

'Faster, faster . . .!' I heard Sir Geraint groan, and he began to answer the lady's humble prayers with eager thrusts into the depths of her warm throat. I rubbed my own shaft harder too, imagining it buried in Estella's mouth, enclosed by her luscious full red lips, teased by the tip of her lascivious tongue. But I was careful not to bring my own crisis too quickly, for my pleasure was extreme and I wished to enjoy every moment of the spectacle laid out before me, with full stones and a good hard prick.

To my immense disappointment, Sir Geraint gave a sudden cry and with a final thrust flooded my lady's mouth. So sudden and abundant was his crisis that Estella was unable to swallow all of his seed, and I saw tiny trails of the precious liquor trickling from the corners of her full-lipped, red mouth.

What a fool I had been to have thought that Sir

Geraint would be as anxious to prolong his pleasure as I was! It would undoubtedly take the knight some time to recover his potency and eagerness, and here was I outside his window, my hand on my throbbing shaft and with all the sport at an end.

But if I had imagined the spectacle to be over, I was very much mistaken. For, to my surprise and delight, Sir Geraint's member rose up as quickly as any young stable lad's under the Lady Estella's expert handling. She stroked and caressed it as though it were some dear pet animal, or a wounded bird dying for lack of warmth and succour. She tended to it most attentively, and it very soon began to flutter miraculously into life, lifting up its head as though it sensed its home was near.

Sir Geraint still lay upon his back on the furs, and he held out his arms to his lover, bidding her to him:

'Come to me, I prithee; ride me.'

And the lady climbed quickly astride her charger, holding her lips apart so that her lover's lance thrust smoothly and speedily into the hot, inviting depths of her belly.

Reaching behind her, she began to stroke his balls, running a teasing fingernail from arse to balls and then cupping them, first very gently, and then more firmly, as she rode her steed. And how merrily she rode him, her breasts bouncing delightfully on her chest and the flesh of her arse spreading out and quivering as the pursuit gathered pace and became a furious gallop. No warhorse ever carried its knight more bravely in the heat of battle than did the noble Sir Geraint, panting and champing at the bit as his mistress spurred him on to victory.

'Faster, sirrah, faster!' she cried. 'For I can see our goal in sight. Do not fail me now!'

And the noble knight obeyed at once, thrusting into her lustily and grasping her thighs as they galloped towards their goal.

And I too could feel the climax approaching. I pumped my shaft harder now, for I longed above all to share in the lovers' ecstasy.

'I die, I die!' cried out the Lady Estella, falling forwards upon Sir Geraint's chest as his thick, creamy sperm foamed out of her and trickled over his balls and thighs.

And with a juddering sigh which dared not turn itself into a cry of ecstasy, I felt my own seed rising in my shaft, spurting out in great torrents over my hand, my wrist. I sank to my knees, dizzy with the sheer delight of it, my head still spinning and filled with the glorious pictures of what I had seen.

I dared not linger long beside the lodge, for I knew that I must reach Redesford before Sir Geraint, and appear to have been there all afternoon.

When at last Sir Geraint brought the Lady Estella to me, dusk was fast closing in and she and I had a long journey before us. We rode in silence most of the way, for I found it impossible to believe that this modest, sweet-faced matronly lady could be the same goddess I had seen frolicking naked in the huntsman's lodge. I gazed sidelong at her, and knew she must have seen my admiring looks, for there was a smile of amusement on her lips. I prayed that she did not suspect that she was being escorted back to her manor by a lad who had just spent the most exciting hour of his life, watching her and her lover disporting themselves in a cottage in the woods.

As we rode in through the gates of her manor, my Lady Estella turned to me and spoke in her soft and subtle voice:

'Alisander, my boy; would you do me a very great service?'

'Anything, my lady. Anything!' My heart was so full of desire for her, that I would indeed have ridden to the very edge of the world for her – aye, and cast myself into the abyss!

'Then I pray you, to go on my behalf to the sisters at the Priory of St Hilda, in the forest. You know of the house?'

'I do, my lady. It is the house by the ford.'

'Then take this package. Mind that you take good care of it. It is to be delivered into the hands of Mother Agnes, none other. Do you understand?'

'I understand.'

And I took my leave of the Lady Estella, first planting a lingering kiss upon her hand.

The next morning, I rode out into the forest once more, taking with me the package which Estella had given me. In three hours I reached the ford, and crossed the river to the house of the Sisters of St Hilda.

One of the sisters was at work in the garden and hailed me cheerfully as she hurried to open the gate for me. I led in my horse and explained that I had come on an errand from the Lady Estella, bringing with me an important package for Mother Agnes.

'Follow me,' replied the sister, who was young and comely despite her work-callused hands, 'and I shall take you to our Mother Superior.'

Mother Agnes was an apple-cheeked woman in her middle years, clearly well formed and buxom under her voluminous robes. I knelt and kissed her hand as she greeted me with a smile. She smelled soft and sweet and warm, and I would willingly have buried myself in the ample folds of her gown – or better still, her bosom.

I handed over the package, which was soft and light, and Mother Agnes thanked me. The nuns offered me refreshment, and then, reluctantly, I left the house. But as I left, I heard giggling and stifled shrieks of pleasure coming from the small building which served as the sisters' dormitory. Also a curious scent . . .

I determined that I would find out what was happening.

When the gates of the priory had closed, and all the sisters were once again inside the house, I left my horse tethered out of sight and waded back over the ford. It was not difficult to gain access to the house by climbing over the wooden palisaded fence, and I dropped down silently into the inner court. My heart was thumping in my chest as I crept to the window of the dormitory and peered inside.

I could hardly believe what I saw within. Five of the sisters were dancing in a circle around a copper brazier, laughing and holding hands. A strangely scented smoke was rising from the brazier, and I saw in the corner, Mother Agnes throwing what looked like herbs on to the fire from the packet with which I had been entrusted by the Lady Estella! The smoke drifted out of the window and into my nostrils, and made my head spin, set my loins aflame with desire . . . all the more so because the sisters and their Mother Superior were entirely naked!

I was gasping with lust and amazement at this new revelation, when I felt cool hands upon my shoulders and turned around with a cry of surprise. Four of the sisters seized my arms and dragged me, too amazed to protest, into the dormitory, to face my punishment at the hands of Mother Agnes.

'So soon returned to us, young Alisander?' Mother

Agnes smiled, as I was dragged panting and dishevelled before her. 'Sisters: what punishment should we decree for this young man whose great pleasure is in watching the enjoyment of others; and who is too timid to take his own pleasure with a woman?'

'Strip him! Beat him! Ride him!' chorused the sisters, still giggling from the effects of the intoxicating herbs which my Lady Estella had so kindly sent them. Nor was I invulnerable to their effects: the fumes seemed to enter my brain, my loins, my very being; and to wash away my every inhibition. For the first time in my life, I felt ready to have congress with a woman. But with nine Holy Sisters and their Mother Superior?

Before I had time to think, hands descended upon me from every angle, and I found myself naked and helpless on one of the narrow beds in which the sisters slept in such sweet harmony, two to a bed. Hands pinned me down. Lips seemed to fasten on every inch of me. Tongues licked at me and teeth nibbled gently, teasing and tormenting my flesh.

I was in a daze of pleasure: as helpless as a babe and yet ramrod-stiff; my only duty or possibility to lie still and allow myself to be petted and preened and adored. My prick reared its head with joy, and I began to groan and hallucinate as the herbs took greater effect.

But I was quite unprepared for what happened next. Those same hands grew rough and ungentle, rolling me on to my front and splaying my legs. A sudden searing pain cut through me, and I realised what was happening to me. The sisters were carrying out their punishment to the letter, and beating me with the cat-o'-nine-tails they used upon themselves and each other for penance and pleasure.

And it was both a penance and a pleasure to me,

also. Now, at last, I realised why the Duc de Montrechatte had been so eager to surrender to Rosilde and her cruel discipline. Waves of exquisite pain surged through my back and backside, and turned almost instantly into a great tide of glorious pleasure. I cried out my pain and joy, but my cries were stifled by the straw-filled mattress on which I lay. My body bucked and sweated under the lash, but all I could think of was the one word, pulsing through my mind again and again:

'More, more, more . . .'

At length, the women ceased beating me and began instead to run their hands and tongues over my back and arse-cheeks, one or two even venturing so far as to wriggle their adventurous little tongues into my arse-hole, which practice caused me agonies of embarrassment, and yet the most exquisite delight.

Then they rolled me over on to my back, and held me fast as Mother Agnes approached, naked and terrifying to my eyes – for she was tall and strong and powerful. And yet I longed to touch those pendulous breasts, to be enveloped in her generous flesh.

Without further ado, the Mother Superior climbed astride me and lowered herself on to my uprearing prick. Despite the pain I felt from the wounds to my back and buttocks, I howled with the sheer ecstasy of feeling her hot and slippery sex sliding down over my prick like a perfectly fitting velvet glove.

She rode me as only a skilled horsewoman can: pumping down on my prick with her powerful thighs, and – to my delight – bending forward so that her breasts hung down and I was able to take one of her nipples into my mouth.

Suckling like a tiny babe, I came to my first crisis

within a woman's belly, and I knew that I should never again fear to follow where my prick led me. As Mother Agnes climbed off me to make way for her sisters to have their way with me, I knew that in my utter subjection and humiliation I must surely be the luckiest man alive . . .

Sir Lyzian

*F*or the first time, the Great Hall echoed to the sounds of knightly laughter, as Alisander blushed and writhed with discomfiture in his chair.

'So!' laughed the sorceress. 'A foolish vice fittingly repaid! I think the payment amply fits the crime – and what is more, I rather fancy you would not mind repeating it!'

The only knight who did not join in the laughter was Lyzian, who had sat silently throughout the proceedings and was the only knight wearing full armour. He was a youthful and comely knight, rosy-cheeked and boyish, with not a trace of stubble upon his beardless chin. Chestnut curls topped his head and he had eyes of the deepest emerald green. He seemed uncomfortable at the turn of events.

'You are very quiet, Sir Lyzian. Tell us, what ails thee?' The veiled sorceress seemed unusually solicitous.

'Nothing ails me, madam.'

'Ah. Then you will not object to telling your own tale to the throng?'

'I have no tale to tell. I am a pure knight. I have deflowered no maidens,' he replied, scornfully. His voice was light and musical.

'My dear Sir Lyzian,' sighed the sorceress, 'I can see that we must needs give you instruction in truthfulness. For is it not true that you do indeed have a tale to tell – a tale of a lady called Ursula and her virtuous sister Brigid: a tale of gratitude and . . . mutual comfort?'

Lyzian shook his head, and would have refused to speak. But at that moment the veiled woman's ringed hand was laid upon his shoulder, and the only thought in his head was of that first, memorable night he had spent with the beautiful girl called Ursula.

And the thoughts turned to words, and came spilling forth in torrents.

THE TALE OF SIR LYZIAN
AND THE LADY URSULA

My virtue is well known among my fellow knights, and throughout the kingdom of Camelot; for my name is unsullied, and the maidens I have rescued have ever testified to my exceptional chivalry and correctness. Never have I laid hand upon any defenceless woman, or done harm to her honour. And most remarkable of all, for reasons which I have chosen not to reveal, no one – man or woman – has ever seen me without my armour. No one, that is, except my chosen companion, the Lady Ursula.

It was a cold and cruel day, and the November

167

wind was cutting through the forest like death with his merciless scythe. 'Twas a day of no comfort for man or beast, and as the dusk approached, the grey sky seemed to press down upon me like a suffocating blanket.

I was out questing in the forest, for all true knights must ride abroad in search of the evil which they are sworn to defeat. In my heart, I hoped that I should soon reach a cottage or manor house, wherein I might beg lodging and food for the night; for despite my armour and thick woollen cloak, I was frozen to the core.

It was then that I heard it: the faint but urgent cry of a woman in distress – and I knew that I must answer her plea for help. Spurring on my trusty steed Troy, I rode in haste towards the source of the sound, deeper and deeper into the thick forest.

At last I came upon a clearing, and there, in the centre of it, I saw a young girl, stripped naked and tied to a tree. Around stood a party of rough-looking villains – five in all, and the face of each one a picture of purest evil. Silently, I reined in my horse and watched for a while, from the shelter of the trees, to get the measure of my opponents.

When they had finished roping the poor girl to the oak tree, and inspecting her delicate white flesh with lustful hands, the brigands began to undress, exposing their erect pricks. Then the tallest of the five, a powerful, scar-faced man whom I took to be the leader of the gang, picked up his discarded belt and signalled to his fellows to follow suit. He then raised his arm up above his head and brought down the makeshift lash with a stinging blow across the girl's breasts, causing a red welt to appear on the pale flesh. With grunts of satisfaction, his fellows now joined in, until the poor lass was in such confusion that she seemed not to know where she was or what was being done to her.

The leader of the brigands laid down his belt and approached the girl, who was by now too terrified to make a sound. He forced apart her thighs with his rough hands and explored her inner moistness with ungentle fingers:

'A virgin, by God!' he laughed. 'But not for long, I'll wager!'

It was clear what they intended to do next with the poor lass, and I – who had sworn a sacred oath as a Knight of the Round Table – could not suffer such a terrible fate to befall any damsel. I therefore spurred on my horse and rode at a furious gallop into the clearing, my sword unsheathed and my dagger at the ready in the other hand.

Seeing my approach, the girl began to cry out once again:

'Sir Lyzian, it is you, I know it is you! Save me, I pray you, good Sir Knight! For my honour and my life are at stake.'

'Fear not, fair damsel!' I replied, swinging about me with my sword and bringing down one of the brigands with a vicious slash to the shoulder. 'I shall save thee.'

But the brigands were not so easily daunted. Although naked, their weapons were laid by, close at hand, and in a moment they were armed to the teeth again, wicked daggers and swords at the ready. A dwarfish fellow with only one good eye was behind me in a flash, clambering up on to Troy's back, and almost having me with a dagger-thrust in the thigh – but I heard the swish of his blade, and wheeled around just in time to fell him with a blow from the edge of my sword, which sent him dazed to the ground.

Two other fellows came at me with evil looks in their eyes, but I ran one through with my sword, and the other took fright and ran off into the woods. This left only two of the villains properly in the fray – the murderous-looking leader and one of his henchmen, a blond giant with a scar running down the left side of his face, from hairline to jaw. A giant, perhaps, but too slow for me – one swift blow from the pommel of my sword, and I had knocked him senseless.

But I had not reckoned with the agility and cunning of the brigands' leader, who ran around behind my horse and pricked his fetlocks with the point of a dagger, causing Troy to rear up and throw me. I fell to the ground, dazed, only half aware of the fact that Troy had finished the work I had been unable to finish, kicking out at the brigands' leader and fetching him a fearful blow to the belly which left him winded and crawling off, powerless, into the woods.

After a few moments, I felt a little stronger, and managed to pull myself to my feet and stagger over to where the terrified maiden was weeping out her gratitude, still lashed to the tree trunk. Taking out my dagger, I slashed through her bonds and released her, noticing – despite my befuddled state – that she was an appetising morsel and indeed a dish fit for any knight's table, or his bed.

But, as the lass fell naked and weeping into my arms, the blow I had received earlier caught up with me and I felt darkness creeping around the edges of my sight. Within moment's the ground rushed up to catch me, and I knew no more.

What passed next, I know only because it was told me by the damsel, whose name was Brigid. Terrified for the life of her rescuer, she had run off into the forest, back to the cottage of her beautiful sister Ursula, who was renowned for her powers as a healer.

She and her sister returned to where I had fallen, bringing with them two strong men of Ursula's village, who were eager to come to the aid of the virtuous knight Lyzian, who had so selflessly rescued young Brigid from a fate worse than death.

I was carried back to Ursula's cottage, where I was put to bed until such time as I might awake from my stupor.

And so it was that I opened my eyes in a strange room, lying in a strange bed and gazing up into the beautiful eyes of a woman whom I had never seen before in my life.

And oh! my stars! I realised immediately what had happened, and that I was no longer wearing my armour! So this strange and lovely woman who was gazing down upon me must know my secret . . .

'Are you Sir Lyzian?' asked the woman, soothing my brow with a kerchief, dipped in a cooling infusion of woodland herbs. 'I am sure that you must be, for I have seen you jousting at the autumn tournaments; and I have heard tell of your great virtue.'

'I . . . Yes, I am Lyzian,' I replied with great reluctance, for in truth I was in great confusion.

'But is it not truer to call you Lyzianor?' enquired the lady, who I confess had already greatly bewitched me with her surpassingly beautiful breasts, which seemed to float and sway in a graceful dance beneath the warm fabric of her winter gown.

'I must have coloured, for the lady smiled and continued:

'Have no fear, Lyzianor; for none knows your secret

save myself. I sent my sister Brigid away before I undressed you, for already I had my suspicions of your true identity. Have no fear, Lyzianor. For none knows but I that you are a woman!'

And so it was that my guilty secret was revealed! All the years of secrecy brought to nought, as in my heart of hearts I had known they must one day be. And my womanhood brought to sight by this lovely woman, whom, and I confess it with trembling lips, I desired beyond desire, beyond any feeling I had ever had for man or woman in my entire life.

'May I know your name?' I asked faintly, for I was still weak.

'My name is Ursula, and I am a healer and prophetess. Through my powers of divination, I knew your true identity even before I undressed you.'

'And shall you reveal my identity to the world?' I asked her. 'For if you do, it will surely bring terrible disgrace upon the Round Table and I shall be cast out into the wilderness in my shame and dishonour.'

'Be still, be still,' the Lady Ursula urged me, clasping my hand to her bosom so that I grew more restless still with an excitement I could not name. 'I wish only to help you, and to be close to you. Lyzianor, it seems to me that there is one way in which you can ensure that no one suspects you are a woman.'

'And what is that?'

'Why, by taking unto yourself a lady. A lady who shares your bed. No one would ever suspect you then.'

'But . . . I am a woman. How can I share my bed with another woman?' I was trying desperately to keep the excitement from my voice. 'And what woman in this world would ever agree to be my bedfellow?'

172

'Why, Lyzianor, I would be honoured to share your bed! Will you not allow me to bring you some comfort?'

And before I knew what was happening, the Lady Ursula began to remove her clothes before me. She was tall and well made; a chestnut-haired goddess with both strength and sweetness, the softness of womanhood and the suppleness of muscle – a thoroughbred mare, and I longed to ride her in my own way: a way which would please both the rider and the steed.

Beneath her midnight-blue gown, Ursula wore no undergarment, despite the cold of the night. As the velvet slid slowly to the floor, I saw her beautiful body in all its magnificence, its perfection: strong shoulders supporting full but firm breasts, rosy-tipped and succulent; a lithe and supple torso, narrowing to a remarkably slender waist and then flaring again into broad, womanly hips. Her thighs were strong and muscular, and I began to wonder what delights were concealed beneath the modest chestnut-brown triangle of her pubic hair.

The Lady Ursula pulled back the covers of my bed, and did not as I had hoped get into the bed beside me. Instead, she sat down on the edge of the bed and began to caress my nakedness wonderingly.

'Such beauty, such strength!' she breathed, running gentle fingertips the length of my flank. 'But tell me, my dear Lyzianor, how came you to take on the outlandish garb of a knight, and hide your comely breast beneath cold iron and burnished leather?'

Though I could scarce think for the great waves of pleasure which were spreading through me as Ursula stroked my flesh, haltingly I told her my tale:

'I was born a wench and yet from infancy my

173

slender frame concealed the heart of a man. I had no interest in girlish pursuits, and as I grew I felt no stirrings within me when men paid me compliments about my budding breasts or swelling hips. On the contrary, I began to realise that the only time I ever felt fleshly pleasure was when I looked upon a comely lass.

'Naturally, such feelings disturbed and confused me; and as I believed that it must be wrong for a girl to desire other women, I set about proving to myself and the world that this shameful fact was not true.

'I set my sights upon the foreman in my father's vineyard; for he was a handsome and powerful man, broad-shouldered and – so I had heard – endowed with the most impressive penis. Since all women desired him, and few had succeeded in turning his head, I told myself that if I conquered him and persuaded him to relieve me of my virginity, I would feel aroused if only through the sense of conquest.

'And so I set about charming the man – Olaf was his name. Although the truth was I felt no desire for him, I preened and simpered whenever he was around and made sure that he realised the nature and extent of my designs. Though by choice I would have worn a jerkin and leggings like the lads I kept company with, I began to wear close-fitting dresses and to wear my bodice cut low so that Olaf would glimpse the swelling fruits within. And to tell the truth, there was some excitement in the pursuit.

'One warm September day, as I was helping to unload the first of the grapes from the vineyard into the huge wooden vat where they would be trodden, I saw Olaf coming back from the vineyard with a basket of grapes. With him was Jana, a small, boyish-looking girl who had often made my pulse race with her sultry looks and suggestive poses – but I had always resisted the call of my heart, for I deemed it shameful. As soon as she and Olaf entered the winery, Jana went off to attend to some of the wine-presses and I completely forgot that she was there.

'Olaf greeted me with a broad smile:

' "Well met, young Lyzianor!" quoth he. "Why, 'tis such a warm day, methinks I and thee are over-dressed!"

'And to my consternation, Olaf strode over to the door of the winery and drew the massive iron bolts across, so that we might not be disturbed. Then he began to undress, stripping off his sweat-stained shirt to reveal a well-formed chest on which grew a profusion of broad hairs, flecked here and there with grey. Then he unfastened the drawstring about his waist and pulled down his leggings. Although I had seen men's pricks many times before – for we were country folk and not coy about such things – I had never seen one erect, nor had I seen one so well formed and thick as this one was. In spite of my misgivings, I began to feel a little excited at the prospect of having such a mighty instrument within my most secret places.

'Once naked, and seeing me apparently paralysed with fright, Olaf turned his attentions to me:

' "What – still dressed, my lass? I'll soon remedy that!" And he set to stripping me of my clothes, as perfunctorily as if I were a tiny child and he my wet-nurse, unwrapping my swaddling bands.

'And so, within moments, I stood before Olaf, naked as the day I was born, and shivering with apprehension. For I cannot in truth say that I felt any great urge of sexual desire for him. At his bidding, I laid myself down upon the beaten earth floor and he knelt between my thighs. After kissing and biting my nipples awhile, he tired of the delay – and of my unresponsiveness – and pulled my thighs wider apart, placing the tip of his weapon against my secret gate and lamenting the dryness of my hole.

'It was at that moment that I caught sight of Jana, who was watching covertly from the shadows. With a start of excitement, I saw that she had pulled down the front of her bodice, and was toying with her own bubbies, which were soft and appetising. At once, I felt an immense wave of desire sweep over me, and a great flood of love-juice filled my belly, moistening my intimate entrance and trickling down on to my thighs.

'Olaf, of course, had no idea that my excitement was coming not from his ministrations but from my sight of another woman's intimacy; and, with a grunt of satisfaction, he pulled apart my lips and rammed his hardness into me. His entry caused me a little pain, but my cries were of pleasure, for as I looked behind him I saw that Jana had sat down, facing me, and was lifting up her skirts. Spreading wide her thighs, she began to toy with her sex, pulling aside the lips so that I should have the best possible view of her merry sport. And all the time, she was running her tongue lasciviously over her lips, as though telling me what she would like to do to me.

'How I gasped with mounting desire as the rough foreman rode me – and how ironic were my cries, for it was not Olaf who was initiating me into the world of pleasure, but that slut Jana, who had now picked up a stout length of broom-handle, and was sliding it with obvious relish into the depths of her dripping wet hole, all the time rubbing at her clitoris

176

with all the vigour of my mother's maid polishing the family silverware.

' "I'll make thee come, little slut!" murmured Olaf in my ear; and indeed I knew that I was about to come – but my orgasm was in no way due to him. For, although it was his prick rubbing away at my clitty, and his hardness inside me, it was Jana that I was looking upon, and Jana I imagined, stroking me with her fingers and licking at me with her tongue, and ramming that long wooden pole up into the very depths of me.

' "I die, I die!" I cried, falling back on to the earthen floor with a great sigh of ecstasy as Olaf pumped his seed triumphantly into my defiled hole. I could have sworn that I also heard another woman sigh with satisfaction, very close by.

'When I recovered my senses, Olaf was on his feet and already half dressed; and there was no sign of Jana. As for me, I felt even more confused than I had done before; for, whilst I had at last received a man's prick within me, I had not enjoyed the experience for its own sake – and my ecstasy had been brought to me by the sight of Jana, lewdly rubbing herself entirely for my benefit.

'I was full of guilt and shame; and, although Jana tried on several occasions to seduce me into her bed, I vowed to myself that I would never take that shameful road, for fear of discovery. And yet, I knew that I could never lie with another man – and so I saw myself condemned to a life of unwilling celibacy.

'Tomboy that I was, I had always longed to be a man and to dedicate myself to the life of a warrior. I had spent many a happy hour with the lads of my father's household, learning with them how to wield both broadsword and lance. And one night, I took a sharp knife and cut off all my long, glossy hair, hacking it close to the scalp. Putting on my brother's garb, I realised with a shock that I could pass for a lad. And a plan began to form in my mind.

'That very night, I rode forth from my father's house in secrecy and never more returned. I took myself to Camelot, where I presented myself as Lyzian, a penniless young squire. Within a few years, I proved myself worthy to be a knight, and that is how I became Sir Lyzian of the Round Table. None but you has ever discovered my secret.'

'Your secret is safe with me,' smiled Ursula, bending to kiss the glossy triangle between my thighs. Instinctively, I parted my legs so that her tongue could wriggle a little way into the furrow which no woman had ever touched, though I had longed for that blissful, sinful touch.

Reaching up, I put my arms around Ursula's wrist and pulled her towards me. Eagerly, she lay down on me and allowed me to kiss her, exploring her smooth white skin with avid fingers, long starved of what they so desired.

'I want you,' I breathed, hardly daring to speak the words; and having spoken them, hardly believing the sound of my own voice, urgent with desire.

'And my desires are all for you,' replied Ursula, who had worked one of her thighs between mine, so that her muscular hardness lay firm against my throbbing clitoris. 'For I, too, have never desired a man. Shall I tell you how I first discovered the joys of womanly love, my dearest Lyzianor?'

I begged her to continue, and as I teased her nipples with my fingers and tongue, she told me her tale:

'My father was the Baron de Guelphin,' she told

me. 'He was a cruel man who abused his power over all who served him – especially his womenfolk. He had unquenchable sexual appetites, and I feared that the *droit de seigneur* extended not only to the village wenches, but also to his own daughters. As I and my sister approached womanhood, we suspected that very soon he would demand that we each become, in turn, his bedfellows. And so we planned that we would each escape from his evil influence.

'My younger sister, Clothilde, succeeded in persuading a rich aunt to take her into her household as a companion; and, unable to find any good excuse, my father was forced to let her go.

'This, needless to say, left me as my father's main target, and I knew that I must somehow escape before he deflowered me. At last I realised that my only course of action was to take the veil; and I announced to my father that I intended to enter the nearby convent of St Winifred. Although enraged at my decision, he was unable to oppose it, for to do so would have brought down suspicion on himself. And so it was that, on my sixteenth birthday, I was admitted as a novice to the convent of St Winifred.

'I had, of course, no true vocation for the veil; but during my time with the sisters, I learned one great truth: that the truest and most exciting love of all is the love of one woman for another.

'One night, not long after I had arrived at the convent, I was awoken in the middle of the night by a knock upon the door of my cell. The door opened, and in came Sister Eloise, a beautiful nun a few years older than myself, who had been extremely kind and attentive to me ever since my arrival. She was wearing only her night-shift, and was obviously cold and shivering.

' "Sister Eloise!" I cried. "Why are you come to me so late in the night?"

' "I am come to bring you comfort," she replied, with a smile. "But first, you must needs warm my flesh. May I get into bed with you?"

'I of course made way for her, and to my great surprise, Eloise took off her shift before getting into bed beside me.

'As soon as I felt her naked warmth beside me, I began to feel the strangest stirrings in my belly, and my nipples grew stiff and started to tingle.

' "My dear Ursula," whispered Eloise. "Your breathing is very hoarse. You must take off your shift and let me massage your chest, to ease the congestion."

'Ever the obedient novice, I of course obeyed; and in truth I was not soothed but greatly aroused by dear Sister Eloise's ministrations – which, of course, was exactly as she had hoped. For I began to return her caresses, exploring her body as she explored mine.

'Gently, very gently, Sister Eloise took my hand and placed it between her open thighs, showing me exactly where to rub in order to give her the greatest pleasure. And you can imagine my delight when, after a few minutes of this delightful occupation, my hand was inundated with her juices as she flung back her head and moaned in ecstasy.

'Now it was my turn to experience the delights of sisterly love. For Eloise knelt between my thighs and began to lap like a she-cat at my most intimate parts. How I wept for joy as she brought me to the peak of ecstasy for the first time in my life.

'We spent that night – and many others – in each other's arms. But I had no vocation for the convent, and when the news came to me that my father had died, I left without taking my final vows and came to live in this cottage, here to continue my mission as a healer, and to protect my young sister Brigid, who was fortunate enough to escape my father's attentions because she was but a child when I left for the convent.'

Our confessions had brought back to our minds a host of remembrances, both fond and fearful; and we fell immediately into each other's arms, there to take both comfort and pleasure.

For the first time in my life, I summoned the courage to explore the depths of another woman; and I found Ursula's womanhood both welcoming and sweet. Her honeydew poured forth on to my lips and I drank deeply of her, coaxing her little pink rosebud into an early blossoming. And for her part, Ursula put her fingers inside me and taught me how joyful the touch of flesh within flesh can be. Our limbs, our tongues, our fingers, met and mingled, and our juices flowed and we fell a-slumbering in each other's arms.

When I awoke, I was surprised to see Ursula up and about, and examining my knightly apparel with rare interest.

'What is this for? And this?' She seemed most interested in my clothing.

'The best way to tell you is to show you!' I replied, and leapt from my bed, now fully restored to health and eager to resume our unarmed combats.

I took the leather jerkin that I wore close against my skin and pressed it against Ursula's nostrils:

'It is full of your scent!' she cried. 'Put it on me, I pray you.'

And I slipped it over Ursula's shoulders, leaving it open at the front so that her breasts were still bare, and following it with the leather hood I wore beneath my helmet, and the leather gauntlets which protected my hands from the harsh chainmail.

Next, I took the breastplate and strapped it on over the jerkin, tightly so that Ursula would be sure to feel the delicious shock of the cold metal against her bare flesh; and I thrilled to feel her shivers of pleasure as I armed her for the fray. The rest of her flesh I left bare, so that I might toy with her more easily; and I soon brought her to her pleasure with the tip of my questing tongue.

'If I am now the knight,' panted Ursula, 'then your sword must now be mine! Therefore I command you, wench, to bend forward over the bed and let me chastise you for your immodesty!'

I obeyed, ensuring that my feet were well apart, for I had no idea of what Ursula intended. Sure enough, no sooner had I bent over the bed and braced myself, than I felt the flat of the sword upon my rump. The sensation was painful but extremely pleasurable, and my sex was soon dripping again with desire for my newfound love.

The next thing I knew, my moistness was being stretched by something cold, hard and smooth – something that was not a penis, and yet was of a similar shape and size. Sudden realisation hit me: Ursula was fucking me with the pommel of my own sword!

The sensation was exquisite: my lover was fucking me, and with the most unusual and delightful prick. And as she slipped her hand round to the front of my body and placed a leather-gloved finger upon my clitoris, I exploded with long-denied pleasure.

At that moment, the cottage door opened, and I saw Ursula's sister, Brigid, standing framed in the doorway. For an instant, my heart sank – it was one thing for my trusted lover Ursula to know my secret, but the girl Brigid would be sure to tell everyone!

But I need not have worried. For the girl closed the door behind her, and ran into the room with cries of delight:

'Oh how wonderful! My darling Sir Lyzian is a woman! May I join in? Oh, please say that I may!'

And no sooner was she in the room that she was stripping off her clothes and baring her flesh, still marked from the ordeal she had suffered the previous day. And I must confess that, much as I am enamoured of my dear Ursula, her sister Brigid is the finest licker a knight could ever wish to meet.

And so it was that I came to be betrothed of the virtuous Lady Ursula, my constant companion and intimate confidante – the ideal consort for the equally virtuous Sir Lyzian. And so it was also that I came into possession of a new squire – a slender, girlish lad it is true, but one whose skills and talents are quite beyond compare.

King Arthur

O f all the revelations that had come to light that
night, none could compare with this latest: a
female knight! And worse: a female knight with the
most unusual affections. Never had Camelot seen
such a terrible outrage to the chivalric code.

'Well, well,' applauded the veiled sorceress. 'You
would indeed make a worthy consort for me, were I
possessed of such affections . . . and who is to say
that I am not?'

'Enough,' cried Sir Galahad, the first to recover his
composure. 'You have heard all our tales. Now you
must choose your victim, and keep the bargain to let
Merlin go free.'

'But, my dear Sir Galahad, there is yet one among
you who has not told his tale.'

'The King? But that is unthinkable!'

'Alas, Sir Knight, the bargain stands only if the King
himself participates in our little game. What do you
say, Your Majesty? Will you tell me your tale?'

The King was silent for many moments. Whilst he

was pondering the question, the veiled tormentor strode impudently towards the steps and ascended them to Arthur's throne, where she settled herself in perfect comfort.

Seeing this last outrage, Arthur was spurred into action:

'Madam, I will share my tale with you. But there is nothing in my past to compare with the tales you have been told this night.'

'Your Majesty,' hissed a voice which seemed to come from inside his head, 'you must not lie. It does not accord well with your position.' And he looked up and saw that the sorceress was by his side once more, her cold hand about to touch his shoulder. 'Pray tell us the tale of the young boy King who enjoyed his victim's widow.'

The icy touch was like lightning searing Arthur's soul, preventing him either from keeping silence or from telling untruths. And so he obeyed what he could not resist.

THE TALE OF KING ARTHUR
AND THE WIDOW MARGAISE

I was but a boy when I came to the throne; untried and still somewhat awed by my position – for I had never dreamed that I might one day become King of this blessed realm. I was also ignorant in the ways of women, for my only experience of carnal pleasures had been through the experiments I had made with other youths when I was but a young squire. Of women's bodies and needs, I knew nothing.

Not long after my ascension to the throne, a terrible rebellion broke out, and my hold upon the empire of

Britain was severely challenged. A number of rebel kings, led by King Lot of Orkney, rose up against my rule and sought to break away from the leadership of Camelot. I knew that if I did not fight for my kingdom, I should soon be king of nothing. And so I led my troops out into battle against the rebel kingdoms.

The campaign lasted many months, and the casualties were fearful. But right prevailed, and in the end there remained only the armies of King Lot against me. It was agreed that there should be one final battle, and that the winner should take all the spoils.

The battle was fought on a grim, grey day when the sky loomed dark even at noon, presaging death and destruction. The fight was a bloody one, and very evenly fought; but when dusk fell, the darkness laid its blanket upon the body of King Lot, whom I had unhorsed and slain in hand-to-hand combat. Seeing their king lying dead, his supporters surrendered to me and I was proclaimed once more the King of all Britain.

Impudent puppy that I was, I was all for cutting off Lot's head and displaying it on a spike outside the gates of his castle, as a warning to others that rebellion against King Arthur would bring death and destruction upon them. But my advisers counselled me to a less bloodthirsty course of action, and so I confined my celebrations to a victory parade of my soldiers from the battlefield to the castle of King Lot.

We entered the castle in a vast array of flaming torches, that lit up our faces like devils and must have struck terror into the hearts of the defeated. Our prisoners rode in silence before us as we crossed the drawbridge and gathered in the main courtyard of the castle, where I called for the dead King's Queen to present herself before me.

Queen Margaise entered the bailey from the door to the keep, and came to me with a grace and dignity which drove me wild with rage, so mighty was my youthful pride. It irked me deeply that the wife of my dead, defeated foe should smile at me so winningly and not tear her hair and weep in my presence.

'Come here,' I commanded her. And she obeyed but I could not help feeling that she did so because she herself wished it, not because I had commanded her to do so. 'And kneel before me.'

'As you wish, Sire.' Her ladies-in-waiting spread a cloth for her on the cobbles and she knelt at my feet; but she did not bow her head, preferring instead, to gaze up at me without fear.

'Lady, I have slain your husband,' I announced with deliberate cruelty. 'And now all that was his is mine. Including you. You are mine to do with as I please.'

'Indeed, Sire.' The cornflower-blue eyes did not waver. In fact, I began to feel as though they were boring into me like daggers.

'You may go,' I told her. 'But I command you to order a great banquet to be prepared for this evening. We shall celebrate my great victory over your vile rebel husband, bastard king of this poor, impoverished realm of Orkney.'

I had hoped that my harsh words would move Queen Margaise to some spirited defence of her husband or his kingdom; but I was bitterly disappointed, for she merely gave a half-smile, rose to her feet and curtseyed.

'All shall be arranged as you will it, your Majesty.' And then she turned and left, walking unhurriedly towards the Great Hall of the castle, there to arrange for the night's celebrations. If there was despair in her heart, I had seen none of it so far; and my victory was beginning to feel a little hollow.

I spent the early evening in the apartments which I had commandeered – the luxurious apartments which had been occupied by the late King Lot. I took off my armour, bathed and had my wounds dressed, and then threw myself on to the big soft bed in which the late King had no doubt often bedded his comely wife.

For Margaise was indeed a toothsome morsel – but was she too rich a sweetmeat for such a callow youth as I? Anger rose in my breast as I thought how the woman had spoken to me, how she had refused to be cowed by me even in the very jaws of defeat. Did she not know that she was my prize, that I might do with her exactly as I chose? Did she not realise that, on a whim, I might throw her to the common soldiery for a whore, and see how much mercy their starving pricks would show her?

I thought of the widow Margaise, and could not deny the attraction I felt towards her. A woman of perhaps thirty summers, she was youthful and yet ripe, in ways which were deeply stimulating to an untried boy who had not yet lost his virginity. Young girls did not appeal to me. But a mature woman such as Margaise . . . I could feel my prick twitching its approval, and I took it out and began to caress it lovingly, judging that I had well deserved some innocent delight after my day's hard-won victory.

I cradled my stones in my left hand, gently teasing their velvet purse with my fingers so that they began to tense and anticipate the sudden outrush of their burden. With my right, I began to pump my shaft, all the while daydreaming about the Lady Margaise: her long, golden hair; her insolent blue eyes; her body, slender yet soft, cold yet infinitely inviting. And I wondered what it would be like to sink my prick into her – to have her spread her legs and submit to me because I was her conqueror.

I pondered on the image of Margaise before me, kneeling on the cold cobbles of the inner courtyard. Only this time, she was not gazing up at me with those insolent, infuriating eyes. Her cornflower-blue eyes were brimming with tears, and were downcast as befitted her new subjection. Everything about her bespoke submissiveness, compliance, humility. I gazed with deep satisfaction upon her bowed head, her clasped hands, the slow tear winding its way down her cheek. I could have kissed her tears away . . .

But I was sworn to a crueller and far more satisfying course of action. Unsheathing Excalibur from its jewelled scabbard, I held it aloft for all to see, and let the torchlight flash from its razor-sharp blade. Although Margaise did not dare lift her eyes, I heard her gasp, and looking down, saw that she was trembling with fear at my feet. With casual cruelty, I took hold of my sword with both hands and lowered it until its point was against the lily-white flesh of her throat. To her credit, she did not flinch, though perhaps that was a sign of fear, too – the fear that any sudden movement on her part might provoke me to anger, or take me by surprise and cause my hand to slip . . .

With a sudden downward slash, I slit Queen Margaise's heavy brocade gown from throat to knee, cutting through the layers of robe and petticoats and baring the delicious flesh below, just as one might slice through the peel of a ripe fruit, the better to get at the juicy flesh within.

'Oh spare me, spare me, my lord!' cried Margaise; but I laughed cruelly, and, kilting my robes around my waist, I pulled out my prick and showed it to her, so that she could admire the instrument of torture which was about to mortify her flesh.

Though she was weeping still, I forced open her lips and inserted my penis into the warm darkness of her full-lipped mouth. Taking her hands, I placed them upon my stones and obliged her to caress me as I took her with long, slow thrusts and defiled her noble throat with my kingly seed.

And then, when withdrew from her and she believed that her torment was at an end, I forced her to the ground, laying her upon her backl and ripping the last vestiges of her modesty from her. And, as she lay trembling beneath me, I saddled up and spurred her on, riding my thoroughbred mare until at last we reached the fence and jumped as one, into the sparkling sunlit air of orgasm.

Coming back to my senses, I realised that I was not, sadly, overseeing my Lady Margaise's ultimate humiliation, but in fact still lying upon the bed in her late husband's apartments. Nevertheless, the image had so excited me that I felt my crisis almost upon me. Pumping my shaft harder, and sqeezing at my stones, I rose towards orgasm and watched with immense pleasure as the sperm flooded my palm – imagining that it was spurting out all over Queen Margaise's insolent face.

I dressed in my finest kingly robes, of purple velvet trimmed with ermine, and determined that I should make a fine show indeed at the night's celebrations.

The Great Hall had been royally bedecked with the bannerets of all my knights, displayed alongside those of the rebel King and his vile henchmen, now my vassals. The bannerets of the defeated knights had been rent in two and presented a sorry sight indeed. All my prisoners were forced to sit at my table in chains and sup with their new overlord, knowing full well that the merest whim might send them to their deaths. I had, indeed, executed a few knights that very afternoon, on the field of battle, for they had been slow in swearing an oath of allegiance to me.

With me, at the high table, sat my most favoured knights and advisers, upon whom I proceeded to bestow new honours and rewards, according each of my favourites some appetising morsel of my newly conquered lands. How it pleased me to see the faces of the conquered knights and barons, as they saw their lands slipping away into the hands of their conquerors, and their own status reduced to that of landless vassals!

And beside me, at the head of the table, sat Queen Margaise: pale but firm-jawed and still defiant. I had hoped that forcing her to sit at my left hand, as though I had already acceded to her husband's position and privileges in more than name, would convince her how low she was fallen; but she accepted the compulsion as though it were a rare honour, and I swear sat beside me as regally as any young king's bride on his wedding night.

I was furious at such resolute defiance; and yet the queen's resilience served only to heighten my desire to subdue her, body and soul. My next game, I felt sure, would drain any remaining colour from her cheeks, and have her on her knees before me, begging for the mercy which I would of course not bestow upon her.

I called upon four sturdy men-at-arms to bring in the royal princesses, Margaise's twin daughters, who were but sixteen summers old. They were very like their mother – tall and golden-haired, but with their father's dark brown eyes. They were attired in their most beautiful gowns – high-waisted dresses in emerald green satin, embroidered with meadow flowers – and were a picture of maidenly purity. I smiled grimly to myself as I considered what was in store for them.

Seeing them led in by rough soldiery, a shadow passed over Margaise's face, but she betrayed none of the terror which she must surely have been feeling. She turned to me and asked me, very calmly and quietly:

'What do you intend to do with my daughters, Sire?'

'Patience, my good Queen Margaise!' I replied, with great good humour. 'A little patience and you shall see.'

Then, turning to my men-at-arms, who in truth had fought like lions, and well deserved their sport, I commanded them:

'You may strip the women, and do whatever you will with them. The Lady Margaise and I wish to be entertained.'

To my immense indignation, the two girls seemed resigned to their fate, and made no attempt to struggle as their gowns were ripped from them and their nakedness exposed to the hungry eyes of a hundred lewd knights and soldiers. Why, I might almost believe that they were accustomed to such treatment . . .

The first girl, Melisande, was already being forced to make the difficult decision as to which of two pricks tasted better – for they were being alternately thrust into her mouth for her delectation. Her sister,

Thisbe, was forced to watch as she was then thrown face down on the ground and greedily buggered by each of the four men in turn. Oh, how she cried out as the thick shafts forced their way through her tender flesh and into her most secret places.

'My dear Queen,' I hissed, leaning to my left to whisper in Margaise's ear. 'Be sure that this is exactly what I intend to do to you!'

But when I looked at Margaise, her face was impassive, and she refused to gratify me with fruitless pleas for her daughters' honour, or her own.

It was, in any case, too late for mercy – for my men-at-arms were hungry for yet more sweet and tender flesh. Already they had Melisande and her sister upon their backs on the rush-strewn floor, legs held wide apart and moist cunnies displayed for all to see. All around the Great Hall, men were taking out their pricks and rubbing them, shouting out words of encouragement to their fellows.

Indeed, so excited was I by the spectacle that I too took out my cock and let him have a sight of the proceedings. How he crowed when I reached out for Margaise's hand and forced her to place it upon my penis, feeling its pulsating hardness in her palm. But still she did not resist me, or try to beg for mercy.

With grunts of satisfaction, the first two men-at-arms lay upon the naked bellies of Melisande and Thisbe, and rammed home their pricks. I was enormously disappointed not to see the girls writhing about, or screaming for mercy. On the contrary, they began to thrust their hips backwards and forwards as though actively enjoying the experience; and when, sated, the men removed their pricks I saw not a trace of blood upon their dripping pricks.

'So!' I cried, turning in rage towards Margaise.

'Your daughters are not even virgins! What sort of a kingdom is it where princesses are become common whores?'

'My dear King Arthur,' replied Queen Margaise, calmly and with a hint of mockery in her voice, 'what kind of King is it who orders his men-at-arms to do what he cannot himself perform?'

Fortunately, Margaise had spoken so quietly that none but I had heard her insolent words. But her continued defiance merely served to strengthen my resolution: before I left Orkney, I would force the queen to submit to me, and take of her that which she seemed happy to sacrifice in her daughters.

That night, I went ill-satisfied to my bed, and lay for a long time in angry silence before at last I drifted off into an uneasy sleep. My thoughts and dreams were all of how I should conquer the rebellious Margaise, and submit her to my lustful will.

I was awoken in the middle of the night, by the sound of the door opening slowly, as though someone were very eager not to be heard. Immediately I reached for Excalibur, which at all times I kept beside me, for my thoughts turned instantly to ambush and murder. There were many in this conquered kingdom who might wish me dead, and the widowed queen, Margaise, had many supporters even now, in the hour of her defeat.

I lay very still in my bed, feigning sleep, and hoping to surprise my assailant with a blow from my enchanted sword. Painfully slowly, the door opened a few inches, just wide enough to admit a shadowy form.

From between half-closed eyelids, I glimpsed the figure, silhouetted for a brief moment as the moon emerged from behind a cloud, and realised, with a start, that I was looking upon the naked figure of Margaise. I saw that she carried no weapon – no dagger, no sword. Did she then intend to poison me? Or bewitch me with her naked beauty?

I swore that I would not be her dupe; and yet, my loins were warming already with desire from that brief glimpse of all that I had so desired to conquer.

She glided nearer to me, and bent over me, planting a gentle kiss upon my forehead, and whispered to me softly:

'Arthur, Arthur: awake! And prove to me that you are a worthy king indeed.'

I opened my eyes and found myself looking into that piercing blue gaze, those ice-blue eyes that glittered with a cold inner fire. And all at once I felt my will fail me. Untried boy that I was, I realised with horror that I was paralysed with terror at the prospect of at last having my desires realised; that, though I desired both to possess and to humiliate this insolent Queen who had so successfully belittled my majesty, I was powerless as a babe at the sight of those steely blue eyes, that swelling bosom, those magnificent tapering thighs.

'Art thou then no king at all, thou man-child?' mocked Margaise, sitting down on the bed beside me and, to my dismay, prising Excalibur from my hot and trembling hand. 'Hast no fire in thy belly, no seed in thy stones?'

I realised at once that I was no match for Margaise; that if I was to enjoy her, it would be on her terms. I could never possess such as she, for there was strength in her beyond kingdoms.

'What then, no word for me?' she smiled. 'Then wouldst thou have me leave thee now, and come no more unto thee?'

'No!' I managed to gasp, hoarsely. 'Stay! I command thee to stay . . .'

'Command?' The note of mockery had returned to the honey-smooth voice. 'Learn this, boy king: thou hast no power over me. Oh, thou canst order me killed – but then I should be no more, and in my very death I should have dominion over thee.'

And she leant over me and pulled the bedcovers down below my waist, exposing the naked, foundering vessel of my flesh and the dancing mast that rose from my helpless loins. As her lips closed about my penis I knew that I was lost forever, her prisoner or her vassal as she chose, and I whispered the words of my damnation:

'I submit to thee. Thou art truly a Queen – for thou rulest me entirely. Therefore I do thy bidding gladly. Only teach me . . . teach me what to do.'

She lifted her head for a moment, and smiled:

'I shall teach thee, boy king. And in return, thou shalt undertake to learn thy lessons well, and to give me and my daughters our freedom. Swear it, upon your mother's life.'

'I swear it.'

And Margaise began the most wonderful night of instruction that I have ever experienced. She fastened her moist red lips about the tip of my poor, helpless penis, and brought me ten times to the point of orgasm, but never beyond. I moaned in an agony of ecstasy as, time and time again, she refused to allow me the moment of ultimate joy.

'Wherefore, wherefore tormentest me so . . .?' I cried, almost weeping with frustration.

'Because you are but a boy, and have still to learn that the greatest and most perfect joys come from long waiting. And also because I wish you to know the power of woman over man, child king. It is a lesson you must never forget . . .'

At last, she began to work upon my prick with a will, rubbing it hard with her right hand, whilst with her left she stroked me gently between the thighs, running her fingertips across my stones and along the furrow between prick and arse. And all the time, she sucked and licked at me, and then – at the moment ordained by her and her alone – I came to the most wonderful climax I had ever known, gushing forth all my youthful arrogance in one great spring tide of love-juice.

I thought that she had exhausted me, so great was the effect of her lips upon my prick; but her powers were infinite. Within moments she had coaxed me with fingertips and tongue, back to the same state of yearning helplessness in which she had held me for so long.

'Now child king, I am going to teach you how to enjoy a woman,' she announced. 'There are many different ways, and I shall show you them all. When you have mastered them all, you can give full satisfaction to a woman, then you may call yourself a man. Perhaps one day you shall also merit the title of King . . .'

She climbed astride me, as though she were a knight and I her charger, bearing her joyfully into the heat of battle. She showed me, with caresses and kisses, and thrusts of her powerful thighs, how to enjoy the greatest pleasure and yet make it last for what seemed an eternity. Then, as soon as she had drained me a second time, she lay down on her back and made me enter her again, bringing me back to hardness by tensing the powerful muscles of her vagina, so that they seemed like a gentle hand, masturbating me to ecstasy.

I came into her again and again, in mouth and vagina and arsehole; and every time she raised me like Lazarus from the dead, and every time I wanted more.

At length, she turned to me and said:

'Boy king, there is something that thou shouldst know. I hated my husband, for although he was a magnificent lover, he was also a tyrant and a traitor. To celebrate my freedom from his thrall, I would take thee to the chapel where he lies in state this night, and ride thee upon the lid of his coffin, so that he may see who is the greater King.'

Though I considered this a gruesome and unnatural wish, I agreed to go with Margaise to the chapel where Lot lay in state. To tell the truth, there was something oddly exciting in the idea of taking her in the presence of her dead husband, and the prospect of gaining a final ascendancy over the vile traitor made my prick twitch with convulsive eagerness.

Wrapping cloaks around ourselves, to ward off the chill night air, we made our way to the mortuary chapel, which was situated in the crypt of the garrison church, within the castle walls. It was an eerie chamber, with a vaulted ceiling which gave the place a horribly oppressive air. The chapel was full of shadows that seemed to act out a silent death dance as invisible currents of air distributed the flames of the candles which stood around King Lot's coffin.

It was a simple wooden coffin, for there had been no time to construct something finer and more fitting for the King of Orkney.

'Thou hast no doubts, no fears?' I whispered, suddenly rather daunted by the prospect of making love on the lid of a coffin.

'None. But first, I must see inside. I wish to say a last farewell to him, for though I hated him, he was my husband.'

Together, we lifted off the lid of the coffin. Inside lay the King's body, still clad in full armour, the visor of his helmet pulled down. He looked exactly as though he was sleeping.

'I must see his face,' whispered Margaise. And she lifted the visor of the helmet.

Her sudden scream sent echoes ringing around the chamber.

'What ails thee?' I cried.

'It is not he!' gasped Margaise. 'It is not my husband the King, but his cousin, Lothar. Lothar must have been wearing my husband's armour into battle . . . But why?'

At that moment, I felt strong hands grip me by the shoulders, and before I knew what was happening my arms had been wrenched behind my back, and tied fast, a gag placed over my mouth to stop me crying out for help.

My trussed-up body was flung to the ground, and a tall and massive figure stepped in front of me.

'Lot!' cried Margaise, her hands to her mouth in horror or wonderment, I could not tell which.

'So, the news of my death did not daunt you, hussy!' he cried, tearing off the cloak which Margaise was still clutching about her shoulders. 'Hardly am I gone, and I see you playing the harlot with this young pup who calls himself a King! Still, I can forgive you, wife, for you were ever a hot-blooded bitch. Say, wife: shall we show this puppy the true ways of the flesh?'

'Yes, husband, yes!' cried Margaise, who seemed to have forgotten her avowed hatred of her husband.

And she began to undress him, tearing at his clothes in an attempt to free his penis.

It was indeed a magnificent weapon: long and thick, with a fair glossy purple helmet that any knight would have been proud to bear. As soon as she had freed it from its prison, Lot picked his wife up in his arms and laid her on her back, upon the body of the dead man in the coffin that should have been his. Then he climbed on top of her, running her through with his prick and crying out:

'And so together we exorcise death! Poor Lothar, he died that I might escape – but he was of no great consequence. And now thee and I shall slit the throat of this young pup, and take back this kingdom that is rightfully mine! Ride, wench, ride, and be glad that thou art still alive!'

And they rode there, in the coffin, upon the body of Lot's dead cousin, as merrily as beasts upon the bodies of their dead prey, and I was sickened to see them rutting amid the stench of death. But, as Lot came to his crisis and his seed flooded into his wife, I saw her arm move beneath him and the sudden flash of a blade. With a terrible cry, Lot fell forward on to his wife's body, and lay still.

For the cunning vixen Margaise had slipped the dagger from Lothar's belt and used it to stab her husband through the heart.

When Margaise had freed me from my bonds, I asked her why she had shown me mercy.

'Because, child king that thou art, thou art still more King than Lot ever was,' she replied with a smile. 'And because thou art still young enough to learn. And what lesson hast thou learned, child king?'

'I have learned of the power of woman over man,' I replied, and I spoke the truth.

'Then grant me one boon.'

'It shall be yours.'

'Grant me this kingdom of Orkney, to rule as thy vassal, and I shall ever be true. In return, I pledge my allegiance lifelong, and also that I shall never tell that thou wert a young pup, too frightened to take his dead enemy's wife. And I pledge also, that whenever thou art in Orkney, thou mayest share my bed and gladly.'

And I confess that I did accept her bargain, and kissed upon it; for in truth I was but a child king, and had many lessons still to learn.

And that is why, to this very day, the widow Margaise rules as undisputed Queen in Orkney, a living testament to the power of woman over man.

Epilogue

*A*rthur hung his head; how could he have been forced into making such a shameful confession? The silence in the hall was oppressive now, each knight realising that there was neither goodness nor purity remaining at Camelot: for both had been a sham, an empty façade covering the filth and degradation within the minds of the knights. And now all knew that their King was no less degraded than they.

It was Lancelot who first spoke, challenging the sorceress to make her decision:

'You have heard all our stories now. Mocked us and robbed us of our dignity. Will you now remember the bargain that you made with us, and choose which of us you shall take to be your vassal? For see, time grows short: Merlin is near death.'

All eyes turned to the corner where Merlin sat at the sorceress's feet, devoted as a pet dog, pawing pitifully at her beautiful leg, and begging for release from the tyranny of his yearning prick. He had aged noticeably during the course of the knights' stories, and was haggard and pale; his breath came in short, painful gasps.

'See how your evil desires have robbed him of his youth and strength!' cried Galahad. 'He dies. And only you can save him.'

'Ah yes, indeed,' agreed the sorceress. 'I can save him or let him die – just as I choose.'

'Why are you doing this to us?' demanded Alisander, struggling in vain to rise from the chair where he sat bound by enchantment. 'And who are you?'

'I came to show to an arrogant king and his unworthy knights how great is the power of woman,' replied the sorceress, echoing the words of Margaise. 'And I believe that I have done so. For each of you has languished in the thrall of his – or her – sexual desires, which only a woman's caresses could release. And, as you can see from my poor slave Merlin, pleasure has its price.'

'But who are you?' repeated Alisander.

'Why, I shall show you,' replied the sorceress. And, raising her hands, she tore the veil from her face.

'Margaise!' cried Arthur, suddenly white with shock and trembling with the power of passion newly reborn.

'No, no: it is my Lade Amide!' cried Galahad, trying to hide his face in his hands, yet unable to conceal the convulsive movements of his stirring prick.

'Ursula . . .' gasped Lyzianor. 'My sweet Ursula . . .'

'Gramercy, she wears the face of the Lady Oruale!' cried Sir Gawain. 'And she has come here to torment me!'

Elaine . . . Gisela . . . Morgana . . . Enid . . . Estella . . . the murmurs spread around the table, weaving a tapestry of wonderment and passion that would not be stilled.

'Aye!' cried the sorceress. 'It is true. For I wear the faces of all women. I am all women to all men, for I am the embodiment of your hearts' desires. Whomsoever you most long for, look into my eyes and you will see her there. Gaze into my eyes, and you are lost, lost and damned forever!'

Too late, the knights tried to avert their eyes from the sorceress's face; but already they were bewitched, entrapped into her diabolical web of seduction and deceit.

'I make my choice!' announced the sorceress, smiling sweetly as she gazed upon her enraptured captives. 'I choose my consort, and my choice is that I shall possess you all!'

And uttering strange words of power which set lightning crackling through the silent hall, the sorceress waved her arms above her head. Suddenly as though distilled from the very substance of the lightning, shadowy forms began to appear from every corner of the hall. Figures at first as insubstantial as gossamer, but then resolving into the shapes of women. Naked and beautiful women, with the bodies of angels and the fiery eyes of devils.

'See what a benevolent tyrant I am!' cried the sorceress. 'For I have brought all your hearts' desires to you – Gisela, Margaise, Ursula, Oruale . . . You see, they are here to serve you, every one. Here to ride you till you beg for mercy and yet cry out for more; here to suck your cocks until you long for death and yet crave one more wave of ecstasy. Here is your fate, my fine fellows: to die slowly in the arms of your hearts' desires, and by degrees to sink into a living death. And each time that blissful death is near, I shall restore you once more to youthfulness, again to endure everlasting agonies of pleasure.

'For henceforth you are enslaved to me: henceforth Camelot is mine!'

And with a laugh of victory, the sorceress touched Merlin upon the forehead and instantly he was restored to youth, his prick still dancing yearningly upon his belly. Then she turned to Arthur, and drew the magic sword Excalibur from its scabbard, delighting in the ease with which it served its new mistress.

'Let the revels begin!' cried the sorceress, lifting Excalibur aloft; and each beautiful phantom seized upon her helpless victim, teasing cock and balls, nipples and belly and arse with tongues and fingers and lips that would never tire.

At last, assuming the face and form of a beautiful demon, the sorceress fell upon the body of her willing victim Merlin, once more to drink at the spring of his ever-renewed desires, and to feed upon the powers which had made her the mistress of Camelot.

The storm stilled, and a distant glimmer of light appeared in the night sky. As dawn broke over the castle, the only sound heard was the groaning of knights never sated, hopelessly enthralled by the sorcery of their own lusts. Who could save them now? Must Camelot crumble forever into ruin beneath the sorceress's evil yoke?

And the snow fell thick and silent over Camelot, forming a soft blanket not quite thick enough to stifle the agonised, ecstatic cries of the knights of pleasure.

NO LADY
Saskia Hope

30-year-old Kate dumps her boyfriend, walks out of her job and sets off in search of sexual adventure. Set against the rugged terrain of the Pyrenees, the love-making is as rough as the landscape.

ISBN 0 352 32857 6

WEB OF DESIRE
Sophie Danson

High-flying executive Marcie is gradually drawn away from the normality of her married life. Strange messages begin to appear on her computer, summoning her to sinister and fetishistic sexual liaisons.

ISBN 0 352 32856 8

BLUE HOTEL
Cherri Pickford

Hotelier Ramon can't understand why best-selling author Floy Pennington has come to stay at his quiet hotel. Her exhibitionist tendencies are driving him crazy, as are her increasingly wanton encounters with the hotel's other guests.

ISBN 0 352 32858 4

CASSANDRA'S CONFLICT
Fredrica Alleyn

Behind the respectable facade of a house in present-day Hampstead lies a world of decadent indulgence and darkly bizarre eroticism. A sternly attractive Baron and his beautiful but cruel wife are playing games with the young Cassandra.

ISBN 0 352 32859 2

THE CAPTIVE FLESH
Cleo Cordell

Marietta and Claudine, French aristocrats saved from pirates, learn that their invitation to stay at the opulent Algerian mansion of their rescuer, Kasim, requires something in return; their complete surrender to the ecstasy of pleasure in pain.

ISBN 0 352 32872 X

PLEASURE HUNT
Sophie Danson

Sexual adventurer Olympia Deschamps is determined to become a member of the Légion D'Amour – the most exclusive society of French libertines.

ISBN 0 352 32880 0

BLACK ORCHID
Roxanne Carr

The Black Orchid is a women's health club which provides a specialised service for its high-powered clients; women who don't have the time to spend building complex relationships, but who enjoy the pleasures of the flesh.

ISBN 0 352 32888 6

ODALISQUE
Fleur Reynolds

A tale of family intrigue and depravity set against the glittering backdrop of the designer set. This facade of respectability conceals a reality of bitter rivalry and unnatural love.

ISBN 0 352 32887 8

OUTLAW LOVER
Saskia Hope

Fee Cambridge lives in an upper level deluxe pleasuredome of technologically advanced comfort. Bored with her predictable husband and pampered lifestyle, Fee ventures into the wild side of town, finding an outlaw who becomes her lover.

ISBN 0 352 32909 2

THE SENSES BEJEWELLED
Cleo Cordell

Willing captives Marietta and Claudine are settling into life at Kasim's harem. But 18th century Algeria can be a hostile place. When the women are kidnapped by Kasim's sworn enemy, they face indignities that will test the boundaries of erotic experience. This is the sequel to *The Captive Flesh*.

ISBN 0 352 32904 1

GEMINI HEAT
Portia Da Costa
As the metropolis sizzles in freak early summer temperatures, twin sisters Deana and Delia find themselves cooking up a heatwave of their own. Jackson de Guile, master of power dynamics and wealthy connoisseur of fine things, draws them both into a web of luxuriously decadent debauchery.

ISBN 0 352 32912 2

VIRTUOSO
Katrina Vincenzi
Mika and Serena, darlings of classical music's jet-set, inhabit a world of secluded passion. The reason? Since Mika's tragic accident which put a stop to his meteoric rise to fame as a solo violinist, he cannot face the world, and together they lead a decadent, reclusive existence.

ISBN 0 352 32907 6

MOON OF DESIRE
Sophie Danson
When Soraya Chilton is posted to the ancient and mysterious city of Ragzburg on a mission for the Foreign Office, strange things begin to happen to her. Wild, sexual urges overwhelm her at the coming of each full moon.

ISBN 0 352 32911 4

FIONA'S FATE
Fredrica Alleyn
When Fiona Sheldon is kidnapped by the infamous Trimarchi brothers, along with her friend Bethany, she finds herself acting in ways her husband Duncan would be shocked by. Alessandro Trimarchi makes full use of this opportunity to discover the true extent of Fiona's suppressed, but powerful, sexuality.

ISBN 0 352 32913 0

HANDMAIDEN OF PALMYRA
Fleur Reynolds
3rd century Palmyra: a lush oasis in the Syrian desert. The beautiful and fiercely independent Samoya takes her place in the temple of Antioch as an apprentice priestess. Decadent bachelor Prince Alif has other plans for her and sends his scheming sister to bring her to his Bacchanalian wedding feast.

ISBN 0 352 32919 X

OUTLAW FANTASY
Saskia Hope

On the outer reaches of the 21st century metropolis the Amazenes are on the prowl; fierce warrior women who have some unfinished business with Fee Cambridge's pirate lover. This is the sequel to *Outlaw Lover*.

ISBN 0 352 32920 3

THE SILKEN CAGE
Sophie Danson

When university lecturer Maria Treharne inherits her aunt's mansion in Cornwall, she finds herself the subject of strange and unexpected attention. Using the craft of goddess worship and sexual magnetism, Maria finds allies and foes in this savage and beautiful landscape.

ISBN 0 352 32928 9

RIVER OF SECRETS
Saskia Hope & Georgia Angelis

Intrepid female reporter Sydney Johnson takes over someone else's assignment up the Amazon river. Sydney soon realises this mission to find a lost Inca city has a hidden agenda. Everyone is behaving so strangely, so sexually, and the tropical humidity is reaching fever pitch.

ISBN 0 352 32925 4

VELVET CLAWS
Cleo Cordell

It's the 19th century; a time of exploration and discovery and young, spirited Gwendoline Farnshawe is determined not to be left behind in the parlour when the handsome and celebrated anthropologist, Jonathan Kimberton, is planning his latest expedition to Africa.

ISBN 0 352 32926 2

THE GIFT OF SHAME
Sarah Hope-Walker

Helen is a woman with extreme fantasies. When she meets Jeffrey – a cultured wealthy stranger – at a party, they soon become partners in obsession. Now nothing is impossible for her, no fantasy beyond his imagination or their mutual exploration.

ISBN 0 352 32935 1

SUMMER OF ENLIGHTENMENT
Cheryl Mildenhall

Karin's new-found freedom is getting her into all sorts of trouble. The enigmatic Nicolai has been showing interest in her since their chance meeting in a cafe. But he's the husband of a valued friend and is trying to embroil her in the sexual tension he thrives on.

ISBN 0 352 32937 8

A BOUQUET OF BLACK ORCHIDS
Roxanne Carr

The exclusive Black Orchid health spa has provided Maggie with a new social life and a new career, where giving and receiving pleasure of the most sophisticated nature takes top priority. But her loyalty to the club is being tested by the presence of Tourell; a powerful man who makes her an offer she finds difficult to refuse.

ISBN 0 352 32939 4

JULIET RISING
Cleo Cordell

At Madame Nicol's exclusive but strict 18th-century academy for young ladies, the bright and wilful Juliet is learning the art of courting the affections of young noblemen.

ISBN 0 352 32938 6

DEBORAH'S DISCOVERY
Fredrica Alleyn

Deborah Woods is trying to change her life. Having just ended her long-term relationship and handed in her notice at work, she is ready for a little adventure. Meeting American oil magnate John Pavin III throws her world into even more confusion as he invites her to stay at his luxurious renovated castle in Scotland. But what looked like being a romantic holiday soon turns into a test of sexual bravery.

ISBN 0 352 32945 9

THE TUTOR
Portia Da Costa

Like minded libertines reap the rewards of their desire in this story of the sexual initiation of a beautiful young man. Rosalind Howard takes a post as personal librarian to a husband and wife, both unashamed sensualists keen to engage her into their decadent scenarios.

ISBN 0 352 32946 7

THE HOUSE IN NEW ORLEANS
Fleur Reynolds

When she inherits her family home in the fashionable Garden district of New Orleans, Ottilie Duvier discovers it has been leased to the notorious Helmut von Straffen; a debauched German count famous for his decadent Mardi Gras parties. Determined to oust him from the property, she soon realises that not all dangerous animals live in the swamp!

ISBN 0 352 32951 3

ELENA'S CONQUEST
Lisette Allen

It's summer – 1070AD – and the gentle Elena is gathering herbs in the garden of the convent where she leads a peaceful, but uneventful, life. When Norman soldiers besiege the convent, they take Elena captive and present her to the dark and masterful Lord Aimery to satisfy his savage desire for Saxon women.

ISBN 0 352 32950 5

CASSANDRA'S CHATEAU
Fredrica Alleyn

Cassandra has been living with the dominant and perverse Baron von Ritter for eighteen months when their already bizarre relationship takes an unexpected turn. The arrival of a naive female visitor at the chateau provides the Baron with a new opportunity to indulge his fancy for playing darkly erotic games with strangers.

ISBN 0 352 32955 6

WICKED WORK
Pamela Kyle

At twenty-eight, Suzie Carlton is at the height of her journalistic career. She has status, money and power. What she doesn't have is a masterful partner who will allow her to realise the true extent of her fantasies. How will she reconcile the demands of her job with her sexual needs?

ISBN 0 352 32958 0

DREAM LOVER
Katrina Vincenzi

Icily controlled Gemma is a dedicated film producer, immersed in her latest production – a darkly Gothic vampire movie. But after a visit to Brittany, where she encounters a mystery lover, a disquieting feeling continues to haunt her. Compelled to discover the identity of the man who ravished her, she becomes entangled in a mystifying erotic odyssey.

ISBN 0 352 32956 4

PATH OF THE TIGER
Cleo Cordell

India, in the early days of the Raj. Amy Spencer is looking for an excuse to rebel against the stuffy morals of the British army wives. Luckily, a new friend introduces her to places where other women dare not venture – where Tantric mysteries and the Kama Sutra come alive. Soon she becomes besotted by Ravinder, the exquisitely handsome son of the Maharaja, and finds the pathway to absolute pleasure.

ISBN 0 352 32959 9

BELLA'S BLADE
Georgia Angelis

Bella is a fearless, good-looking young woman with an eye for handsome highwaymen and a taste for finery. It's the seventeenth century and Charles II's Merrie England is in full swing. Finding herself to be the object of royal affections, Bella has to choose between living a life of predictable luxury at court or following her desire to sail the high seas – where a certain dashing young captain is waiting for her.

ISBN 0 352 32965 3

THE DEVIL AND THE DEEP BLUE SEA
Cheryl Mildenhall

A secluded country house in Norfolk is the setting for this contemporary story of one woman's summer of sexual exploration. Renting a holiday home with her girlfriends, the recently graduated Hillary is pleased to discover that the owner of the country estate is the most fanciable man in the locale. But soon she meets Haldane, the beautifully proportioned Norwegian sailor. Attracted by the allure of two very different men, Hillary is faced with a difficult decision.

ISBN 0 352 32966 1

WESTERN STAR
Roxanne Carr

Maribel Harker is heading west, and she's sure grown up since the last wagon train moved out to California. Dan Cutter is the frontiersman that Maribel's father has appointed to take care of his wilful daughter. She is determined to seduce him – he is determined not to give into temptation. Thrown together in a wild and unpredictable landscape, passions are destined to run high!

ISBN 0 352 32969 6

A PRIVATE COLLECTION
Sarah Fisher

Behind an overgrown garden by the sea, a crumbling mansion harbours a tantalising secret: a remarkable collection of priceless erotica belonging to a fading society beauty and her inscrutable chauffeur. When writer Francesca Leeman is commissioned to catalogue the collection, she finds herself becoming embroiled in a three-way game of voyeurism and mystery.

ISBN 0 352 32970 X

NICOLE'S REVENGE
Lisette Allen

Set against the turmoil of the French Revolution, opera star Nicole Chabrier faces a life of uncertainty now that angry hordes are venting their wrath on the aristocracy. Rescued by a handsome stranger and taken to a deserted palace, Nicole and her insatiable lover, Jacques, seek a reversal of their fortune using charm, sexual magnetism and revenge!

ISBN 0 352 32984 X

UNFINISHED BUSINESS
Sarah Hope-Walker

As a financial analyst for a top London bank, Joanne's life is about being in control. But privately, her submissive self cries out to be explored. She has tried to quell her strange desires, but they insist on haunting her. There is only one place where she can realise her desire to be dominated: the *Salon de Fantasie*, run by her enigmatic Parisian friend, Chantal, Soon, the complexities of Joanne's sexuality begin to take over the rest of her life.

ISBN 0 352 32983 1

April 1995

CRIMSON BUCCANEER
Cleo Cordell

Fiery noblewoman Carlotta Mendoza is cheated out of her inheritance by the corrupt officials of Imperial Spain. But help is at hand in the form of a rugged young buccaneer who introduces her to a life of piracy and sexual adventure. Carlotta is determined to make her enemies squirm with shame as she takes her revenge.

ISBN 0 352 32987 4

LA BASQUAISE
Angel Strand

The scene is 1920s Biarritz. Oruela is a modern young woman who desires the company of artists, intellectuals and hedonists. Jean is her seemingly devoted lover who will help her to realise her wildest dreams. But when she is accused of murdering her cruel father, Oruela's life is thrown into turmoil. Bizarre characters play games of sexual blackmail against a background of decadence.

ISBN 0 352 329888 2

May 1995

THE LURE OF SATYRIA
Cheryl Mildenhall

Satyria is a mythical land of debauchery and excess: a place where virtuous maidens dare not venture. When Princess Hedra's castle is threatened with invasion, she takes refuge in this land and finds plenty of virile suitors willing to make her feel welcome. When she is captured by the leather-clad King of Satyria, her lascivious talents are really put to the test.

ISBN 0 352 32994 7

THE DEVIL INSIDE
Portia Da Costa

One morning, the usually conventional Alexa Lavelle wakes up with a dramatically increased libido and the gift of psychic sexual intuition. In order to satisfy strange new desires, she finds herself drawn to an exclusive clinic where an enigmatic female doctor introduces her to some very interesting people. A world of bizarre fetishism and erotic indulgence is about to unfold.

ISBN 0 352 32993 9

BLACK
lace

WE NEED YOUR HELP . . .
to plan the future of women's erotic fiction –

– and no stamp required!

Yours are the only opinions that matter.
Black Lace is a new and exciting venture: the first series
of books devoted to erotic fiction by women for women.

We're going to do our best to provide the brightest,
best-written, bonk-filled books you can buy. And we'd
like your help in these early stages. Tell us what you
want to read.

THE BLACK LACE QUESTIONNAIRE

SECTION ONE: ABOUT YOU

1.1 Sex (*we presume you are female, but so as not to discriminate*)
     are you?
        Male   ☐   Female   ☐

1.2 Age
        under 21   ☐   21–30   ☐
        31–40   ☐   41–50   ☐
        51–60   ☐   over 60   ☐

1.3 At what age did you leave full-time education?
        still in education   ☐   16 or younger   ☐
        17–19   ☐   20 or older   ☐

1.4 Occupation _____

1.5 Annual household income
    under £10,000 ☐   £10-£20,000 ☐
    £20-£30,000 ☐   £30-£40,000 ☐
    over £40,000 ☐

1.6 We are perfectly happy for you to remain anonymous;
    but if you would like us to send you a free booklist of
    Nexus books for men and Black Lace books for Women,
    please insert your name and address

    _____

    _____

    _____ _____

    _____

SECTION TWO: ABOUT BUYING BLACK LACE BOOKS

2.1 How did you acquire this copy of *The Senses Bejewelled*
    I bought it myself ☐   My partner bought it ☐
    I borrowed/found it ☐

2.2 How did you find out about Black Lace books?
    I saw them in a shop ☐
    I saw them advertised in a magazine ☐
    I saw the London Underground posters ☐
    I read about them in _____
    Other _____

2.3 Please tick the following statements you agree with:
    I would be less embarrassed about buying Black
    Lace books if the cover pictures were less explicit ☐
    I think that in general the pictures on Black
    Lace books are about right ☐
    I think Black Lace cover pictures should be as
    explicit as possible ☐

2.4 Would you read a Black Lace book in a public place – on
    a train for instance?
    Yes ☐   No ☐

SECTION THREE: ABOUT THIS BLACK LACE BOOK

3.1 Do you think the sex content in this book is:
     Too much   ☐   About right   ☐
     Not enough   ☐

3.2 Do you think the writing style in this book is:
     Too unreal/escapist   ☐   About right   ☐
     Too down to earth   ☐

3.3 Do you think the story in this book is:
     Too complicated   ☐   About right   ☐
     Too boring/simple   ☐

3.4 Do you think the cover of this book is:
     Too explicit   ☐   About right   ☐
     Not explicit enough   ☐

Here's a space for any other comments:

SECTION FOUR: ABOUT OTHER BLACK LACE BOOKS

4.1 How many Black Lace books have you read?   ☐

4.2 If more than one, which one did you prefer?

4.3 Why?

SECTION FIVE: ABOUT YOUR IDEAL EROTIC NOVEL

We want to publish the books you want to read – so this is your chance to tell us exactly what your ideal erotic novel would be like.

5.1 Using a scale of 1 to 5 (1 = no interest at all, 5 = your ideal), please rate the following possible settings for an erotic novel:

Medieval/barbarian/sword 'n' sorcery ☐
Renaissance/Elizabethan/Restoration ☐
Victorian/Edwardian ☐
1920s & 1930s – the Jazz Age ☐
Present day ☐
Future/Science Fiction ☐

5.2 Using the same scale of 1 to 5, please rate the following themes you may find in an erotic novel:

Submissive male/dominant female ☐
Submissive female/dominant male ☐
Lesbianism ☐
Bondage/fetishism ☐
Romantic love ☐
Experimental sex e.g. anal/watersports/sex toys ☐
Gay male sex ☐
Group sex ☐

Using the same scale of 1 to 5, please rate the following styles in which an erotic novel could be written:

Realistic, down to earth, set in real life ☐
Escapist fantasy, but just about believable ☐
Completely unreal, impressionistic, dreamlike ☐

5.3 Would you prefer your ideal erotic novel to be written from the viewpoint of the main male characters or the main female characters?

Male ☐   Female ☐
Both ☐

5.4 What would your ideal Black Lace heroine be like? Tick
     as many as you like:

Dominant	☐	Glamorous	☐
Extroverted	☐	Contemporary	☐
Independent	☐	Bisexual	☐
Adventurous	☐	Naive	☐
Intellectual	☐	Introverted	☐
Professional	☐	Kinky	☐
Submissive	☐	Anything else?	☐
Ordinary	☐		

_____

5.5 What would your ideal male lead character be like?
     Again, tick as many as you like:

Rugged	☐		
Athletic	☐	Caring	☐
Sophisticated	☐	Cruel	☐
Retiring	☐	Debonair	☐
Outdoor-type	☐	Naive	☐
Executive-type	☐	Intellectual	☐
Ordinary	☐	Professional	☐
Kinky	☐	Romantic	☐
Hunky	☐		
Sexually dominant	☐	Anything else?	☐
Sexually submissive	☐		

_____

5.6 Is there one particular setting or subject matter that your
     ideal erotic novel would contain?

_____

SECTION SIX: LAST WORDS

6.1 What do you like best about Black Lace books?

_____

6.2 What do you most dislike about Black Lace books?

_____

6.3 In what way, if any, would you like to change Black
     Lace covers?

_____

6.4 Here's a space for any other comments!

_____
_____
_____
_____

Thank you for completing this questionnaire. Now tear it out of the book – carefully! – put it in an envelope and send it to:

Black Lace
FREEPOST
London
W10 5BR

No stamp is required!